by Eliza Willard

Based on the motion picture screenplay by
Emily Fox and Adam Cooper
& Bill Collage
Story by Emily Fox

HarperEntertainment
An Imprint of HarperCollins*Publishers*

A PARACHUTE PRESS BOOK

**PARACHUTE
PRESS**

 **DUALSTAR
PUBLICATIONS**

Parachute Publishing, L.L.C.
156 Fifth Avenue
New York, NY 10010

Dualstar Publications
1801 Century Park East
12th Floor
Los Angeles, CA 90067

☕HarperEntertainment
An Imprint of HarperCollins*Publishers*
10 East 53rd Street, New York, NY 10022

Copyright © 2004 Dualstar Entertainment Group, Inc.
All rights reserved.

All photography copyright © 2004
Dualstar Entertainment Group, Inc. All rights reserved.

© 2004 Warner Bros. Entertainment Inc.

NEW YORK MINUTE and all related characters and elements are
trademarks of and © Warner Bros. Entertainment Inc. (s04)

Book created and produced by Parachute Publishing, L.L.C., in
cooperation with Dualstar Publications, a division of Dualstar
Entertainment Group, Inc., published by HarperEntertainment,
an imprint of HarperCollins Publishers.

For information address HarperCollins Publishers Inc.,
10 East 53rd Street, New York, NY 10022.

ISBN 0-06-059509-4

HarperCollins®, ☕®, and HarperEntertainment™ are trademarks of
HarperCollins Publishers Inc.

First printing: May 2004

Printed in the United States of America

www.mary-kateandashley.com

Visit HarperEntertainment on the World Wide Web at
www.harpercollins.com

10 9 8 7 6 5 4 3 2 1

1

Tick, tick, tick. *That's all I can hear. A clock ticking, quietly at first, then louder and louder . . .* Tick tick tick . . . *So loud it seems to echo inside my head.*

Then I see where the sound is coming from— a giant clock. A clock as big as a house. I stare at it, confused. I blink and swallow hard. I'm all out of breath, but I don't know why. What time is it? I stare at the clock, but I can't read it. What do the dots mean? What do those long and short arms mean? I can't remember. . . .

The clock disappears, and I'm in a long white hallway lined with unmarked doors. It's so cold I can see my breath. . . . I walk down the hallway slowly. My feet feel like lead. Come on, move! *I tell my feet.* Time's running out! I've got to get there soon! *Where? I don't know. But I know I have to hurry.*

A bald man in a white suit approaches me and sticks his face right up into mine. All I can see are his lips, which move slowly, as if stuck together with gum. His low voice growls, "I hope you're prepared for your speech."

His breath is metallic and cold. I step away from him. He looks me up and down and stifles a laugh. Why is he looking at me that way? What's so funny?

"Weirdo," I say, and he vanishes.

I keep walking down the hall, looking at the rows of doors. I need to open one of them, but which is the right one? I reach for a door on my left and turn the knob. Is this the way to the auditorium? I wonder. I open the door.

"Arf, arf, arf!" The room is endless, white, and full of barking, yapping dogs. I hate dogs! I slam the door shut. Not the right room.

I drag my weighted feet down the hall. A woman, also dressed in white with a helmet of stiff blond hair, appears out of nowhere. "Looking forward to hearing your speech, Jane," she says.

I pull back from her. "It's a good speech," I say. "Really."

The woman's eyes travel from my head to my feet and back again. She laughs. Why? Why do people keep laughing at me?

Forget it. I've got to find the auditorium. That's the most important thing. I can't be late!

I open a door on the right. My twin sister, Roxy, stands there, waving at me. What is she doing there?

"Are you sure you haven't forgotten something?" Roxy asks. She giggles and slams the door shut.

Forgotten something? What is Roxy talking about?

I see a door at the end of the hallway. It glows with a supernatural light. That must be the door I need! At last I reach the glowing door and open it. My eyes are flooded with blinding light. Where am I? Is this it?

I step forward, blinking. My hands grip a wooden podium. I stare into the light. I'm on a stage, a huge crowd in front of me. They're whispering, pointing at me, and laughing!

"What?" I shout. "What is it? What's wrong with everyone?"

Then I look down at myself, and I understand. Roxy was right—I did forget something. My clothes!

I'm naked!

The laughter rings in my ears, loud and harsh. I try to cover myself with my arms. I open my mouth to scream—but instead of a scream, out comes a loud BUZZZZZZZZZ. . . .

Jane Ryan's eyes snapped open as she sat up in bed, drenched in a cold sweat. The clock radio on the nightstand next to her was buzzing.

She felt for her glasses, put them on, and looked around. She was in bed in her neat pink room in her cozy house on Long Island, New York. She wasn't naked after all—she was wearing her well-starched blue cotton nightgown. There was no giant clock, no cold white hallway, no podium, no mocking audience. . . . She started to catch her breath.

"It's okay," she told herself. "It was just a dream. Just a really, really bad dream."

She slapped a button on the clock radio and the buzzing stopped. Then she picked up her alarm watch, which she wore every day. It was programmed to beep at certain times to remind her of important things she had to do. And today was full of important things. The most important of all—she was a finalist for the McGill Fellowship. The finals would take place that afternoon at Columbia University.

First prize was a four-year scholarship to Oxford University in England. Jane had dreamed of going to Oxford University her whole life and had worked her butt off for the last three years preparing for this moment. This day. Her whole future hinged on how well she did on her speech that afternoon. No wonder she was having nightmares about it.

As long as she nailed her speech, the rest of it was taken care of. She was a straight-A student, student body president, captain of the cheerleading squad, debate champion, and chairperson of the Young Republicans of South Side High School—among many other honors and responsibilities. These activities weren't a chore for Jane. She enjoyed them—and she reached for excellence in everything she did.

Jane glanced at her watch. 7:01. Time to start her morning routine. She got out of bed and headed downstairs to the kitchen.

In the hallway she passed a row of family photos. She stopped to give them each a fond look. Jane and her twin sister, Roxy, age two, with their mother and father on Christmas. The twins at age four on a ski trip with their parents. Halloween, age seven—Roxy dressed as Catwoman and Jane as Tinkerbell. Jane smiled and touched the photo lightly. Their mom had made those costumes for them. Happy times.

The next picture showed last Christmas, when Jane and Roxy were sixteen. They stood in front of the tree with their father, trying to smile. No Mom in sight. Jane sighed. It was the saddest Christmas she could remember.

Her mother had died two years ago. Jane still missed her every day. She'd kept herself busy with activities and schoolwork, which helped keep the sadness away, helped her not to think about Mom so much. She liked to have everything under control, and she took care of her father and sister the way her mom used to. Mom would have wanted that.

The last picture was a portrait of Mom. She was beautiful, blond and blue-eyed like Jane and Roxy, with creamy skin, a warm smile, and a twinkle in her eyes. Jane kissed the photo and said, "Morning, Mom," just as she always did. Then she went into the kitchen.

The kitchen smelled of fresh-brewed coffee. Jane poured a cup from the automatic coffee maker and headed back up the stairs. She met her father, Dr. Andrew Ryan, an obstetrician, stumbling groggily down the hall. His clothes were rumpled and his graying hair tousled. Clearly, he had been up late the night before at the hospital.

"Morning, Dad," Jane said, handing him the coffee.

"Morning, Jane," her father said and gave her a kiss. "Thank you."

On to Roxy's room. Jane opened the door and tiptoed in. It was dark, but Jane could hear Roxy breathing under the covers.

Roxy's room was very different from Jane's. Where Jane's room was tidy and organized, Roxy's looked as if a tornado had passed through it. Ripped jeans, vintage T-shirts, and a flip-flops littered the floor. The walls, painted orange, were covered with rock-and-roll posters, and a five-piece drum kit was set up in one corner of the room.

Jane tiptoed to the bed and threw back the covers. Just as she thought. Roxy was sleeping like a baby, clutching a drumstick and wearing headphones. Every night she fell asleep with music blasting into her ears. Jane didn't know how her sister could do that.

She walked over to the stereo and pressed Play. She watched Roxy to see if she woke up. Nothing. Roxy didn't move a muscle.

Jane slowly turned the volume up, higher, higher . . . Nothing! Finally she cranked it as high as it would go. How could Roxy stand it?

Roxy still didn't open her eyes, but she muttered, "Okay, I'm up."

Jane nodded and smiled. Mission accomplished. She crossed their shared bathroom back to her orderly pink room and opened her closet. Jackets, skirts, crisp shirts, and pants hung in color-coordinated rows. She skimmed through them, looking for the perfect outfit for her McGill Fellowship presentation. Something conservative, yet energetic . . .

She picked out a floral pink suit and white blouse—the same outfit she'd worn on the day she had convinced the South Side High principal that their school *needed* a Young Republicans club. Maybe it would bring her luck.

She had a few minutes left to practice her speech, so she sat at her vanity table and opened her day planner.

Ah, her day planner. The most important thing she owned. It had her whole life in it:

her money, her credit card, her Junior Honor Society membership card, her calendar and her to-do lists. And most important of all, it held a pile of color-coded note cards with the speech she'd prepared for the McGill committee neatly outlined on them.

Jane sat up straight, looked at herself in the vanity mirror, and began to practice her speech. "Ladies and gentlemen, my name is Jane Ryan. . . ."

No, that wasn't quite right. She started over again. "My name *is* Jane Ryan." No, still not right. "My name is *Jane Ryan* and I'm here today as a finalist for the McGill Fellowship."

Perfect. Her alarm watch beeped. Uh-oh. Time for her shower.

"Morning, schmorning," Roxy grumbled. She wasn't what you'd call a morning person. She was barely even an afternoon person. She dragged herself out of bed and put on a black Metallica T-shirt, jeans, and a studded leather wristband.

Her computer beeped, and she glanced at the screen. Cool, an E-mail from her friend Justin DeMarco. She sat down to read it.

From: Justin007
Subject: LIFE-CHANGING EXPERIENCE
Rox—Just got a tip. Simple Plan video
shoot at noon. NYC—59th St. & 9th Ave.

Excellent, Roxy thought. *I'm there*. She loved the rock band Simple Plan, and she knew what Justin was thinking. Her band had just made a demo CD, and this was a great chance to pass it along to a record company executive. Maybe they'd even cast her as an extra in the video!

There was just one teensy-weensy little problem. It was a school day. They kind of expected Roxy to be there.

Jane was excused because of her McGill Fellowship thing. Roxy would just have to find her own excuse. She clicked open a file on her computer. Ever since her mom died, school just didn't seem that important to Roxy. If people wanted to get all bent out of shape about it that was their problem.

Someone knocked at her bedroom door. "*Entrare!*" Roxy called, practicing her Italian.

Her dad stuck his head into her room. "Just wanted to make sure you're up," he said.

"I'm proofreading my English essay," Roxy lied with a slight pang of guilt. No need for Dad to get involved in this. What he didn't know wouldn't hurt him, and Roxy never wanted to hurt her dad.

"Good," he said. "I like what I'm seeing, Roxy. Three weeks into your senior year and you haven't cut school once. Keep it up and we won't have to send you to Sister Mary Margaret's convent school." He smiled and left, closing the door behind him.

Roxy shuddered. Convent school! What a nightmare!

She imagined herself in an itchy school uniform in a room full of supercheerful girls. No way. She'd never fit in at Sister Mary Margaret's. Of course, if she got caught skipping school just one more time, South Side was going to expel her—kick her out on her butt. Then she'd have no choice but to go to the convent.

Well, that's just not going to happen, Roxy told herself. She had whole files of perfectly good excuses stored on her computer. She zipped through them: Illnesses, Family Emergencies, U.S. Holidays, Foreign Holidays, Religious Holidays, Female Problems. . . .

"What excuse should we use this time, Ringo?" Roxy asked. She glanced over at the cage where she kept Ringo, her beloved three-foot-long pet python.

Uh-oh. The cage was empty.

Roxy heard the shower running in the bathroom that connected her room to Jane's. A second later she heard a shriek.

Ringo, Roxy thought. *Why does he love the shower so much?*

The bathroom door jerked open. Jane's wet hands emerged into Roxy's room, holding Ringo by the neck.

"Sorry," Roxy said. She gently took Ringo out of Jane's hand. Jane slammed the bathroom door. What was Jane's problem? Ringo wouldn't hurt a fly. Well, actually, she'd seen him eat flies, but he'd never bother a *person.* . . .

"There you are," Roxy said, cuddling the python. "Aw, Ringo, you're shaking. Did Janey scare you? It's okay, Mommy's here."

She draped Ringo around her neck and went back to her computer. *Hmm . . . feels like a chicken pox day to me*, she thought. She found her pre-written chicken pox excuse note and printed it out.

"There, that's taken care of," she said. "Now it's time for a little practice on the old drums."

She sat at her drum kit and banged out some beats, her blond hair shaking wildly around her head. She loved playing the drums—it helped her release all her nervous energy. Cymbals, snare, high hat, bass—*boom*, *boom*, *boom*, *bam!* She jumped to her feet, raised her arms and shouted, "Thank you, New York!"

Her stomach rumbled. "All right, time for breakfast," she said to herself, heading for the kitchen. "I could really use a Red Bull."

Jane, freshly showered, walked into the kitchen and set her day planner on the table. She glanced at the newspaper Roxy was reading. The headline read, MUSIC PIRATES STRIKE AGAIN. MILLIONS LOST ON COUNTERFEIT CDS.

"You know, the more these guys rip off the music business, the harder it's going to be for new bands like mine to break in," Roxy said.

"Maybe you should choose a more sensible profession," Jane suggested. "Something not so hard to get into."

13

"Like what?" Roxy asked.

Jane paused. To be honest, she couldn't imagine Roxy growing up to be anything but a rock drummer. "Never mind," she said. It didn't matter. The music pirates were not her problem. She had plenty of other things to worry about. She made a beeline for the fridge and opened it.

Let's see, Jane thought as she pulled what she needed from the fridge. *Granola, fresh fruit, and yogurt for Dad* . . . She quickly prepared Dad's breakfast and set it on the table. *And Cocoa Puffs and Red Bull for Roxy.* Jane clucked her tongue in disapproval. Roxy's breakfast was full of sugar, but there was no arguing with her. Jane gave her sister the breakfast she wanted.

"Thanks," Roxy said, digging in.

Then Jane made herself some plain oatmeal, sprinkled a few raisins on it, and sat down to eat.

"How's it going, guys?" Dr. Ryan asked as he walked in, tightening the knot on his tie.

Jane beamed at him. "Great, Dad. Breakfast is on the table."

Roxy looked up from her cereal bowl and smiled at him too.

As their dad sat down to his breakfast, Jane reached for her planner and opened it. Every minute of her day was carefully plotted out. She'd highlighted the most important moment: 3:00 PM McGILL FELLOWSHIP PRE-SENTATION.

A scrap of yellow stuck out from the next page. What was that? Jane turned the page. A yellow Post-it note was stuck on the next day's to-do list under *floss teeth* and *rearrange sock drawer*. It said, *Remove stick from butt.*

Roxy, Jane fumed. What did she have against Jane's day planner? She was always making fun of it. "*Never* touch my day planner," Jane warned Roxy.

"You need to chill on the nerd book," Roxy shot back.

Roxy didn't understand. Jane *needed* her planner. They all did. If Jane didn't keep them organized, the family might fall apart!

Beep, beep! Dr. Ryan's beeper went off. He frowned, checked the number, and reached for the phone.

Jane sighed. She knew what was coming. Another patient was going into labor. Dad could be tied up for hours. He had promised to go up to Columbia University to hear her

McGill speech that afternoon. But what could he do? His patients needed him too.

"Hi, it's me," Dr. Ryan said into the phone. "How far apart are the contractions? All right, tell them to come to the hospital. I'll see them in an hour."

He hung up the phone and turned to Jane. "Honey, your speech," he said, a concerned look on his face.

Jane hid her disappointment. "Don't worry about it, Dad. It's fine."

"No, it's not fine," he said. "Today's your big day. I'm going to do my best to make it up to Columbia this afternoon. But I have to say it doesn't look good."

Jane hugged him. "I'll understand if you can't make it, Dad. You're the best."

"Hey, I don't mean to rain on this touching moment, Dad, but I need your signature on my permission slip," Roxy said. She held out a parental consent form on official South Side High School stationery. Typed into the blank was FIELD TRIP: SHAKESPEARE IN THE PARK.

Jane knew there was no field trip scheduled that day, but she wasn't going to tell on her sister—if Roxy wanted to get kicked out of school, that was her business.

"Shakespeare in the Park?" Dr. Ryan said. "Which play?"

"It's the one with the . . . you know, the one with the guy in tights, and he likes the . . . the . . . girl," Roxy stammered.

Jane rolled her eyes. Roxy had this down to a science. A very inexact science.

"*Romeo and Juliet*?" he said.

Roxy slapped him on the back. "Bingo, Dad."

Dr. Ryan signed the note. "Okay, I've got to run. Roxy, do you mind giving your sister a ride to the train station?"

Roxy sighed. "Fine."

She doesn't have to act so put out, Jane thought. It wasn't as if she had to rush off to school or anything.

Dr. Ryan kissed Roxy on the cheek, then Jane. Then he grabbed an orange and headed out. "Love you guys!" he called.

"Love you too, Dad!" Jane and Roxy called back.

They sat and ate in silence until they heard his car pull away. Then Roxy pulled out her phony excuse form, lined it up under the consent form her dad had just signed, and traced his signature.

"Hope you don't get caught," Jane said. She couldn't keep a note of primness from her voice.

"I won't," Roxy said, mimicking Jane.

Roxy stuck the excuse letter into the countertop fax machine, dialed the school fax number, and pressed Send.

Jane shook her head. Enough of this non-sense. "Come on, let's go. I've got a train to catch."

"No problem." Roxy grabbed her car keys and they headed out to Roxy's ancient, beat-up Volkswagen Beetle with the license plate that read 2QL4SQL.

Jane got in and leaned back against the headrest. She felt something catch in her hair and sat up. A Simple Plan sticker had peeled off the seat and stuck to her head. Ugh. She ripped it off and set it on the dashboard.

A ride in Roxy's car was not complete without sitting on trash, catching your clothes on something sharp, or pulling some-thing sticky out of your hair.

Roxy started the car. It chugged and putted loudly.

"You might want to think about buying a new muffler," Jane shouted over the noise.

"And you might want to think about buying your own car," Roxy snapped back.

"I'm saving for college so Dad doesn't have to pay for all of it," Jane replied. "Of course, if I win the McGill Fellowship I won't have to worry about that. Mind putting on the radio?" It was more noise, but at least it would help drown out the engine.

"Sure thing." Roxy slammed her iPod into its cradle and a Simple Plan song blared through the speakers.

"Don't drive too fast!" Jane warned.

Roxy slammed her foot on the gas pedal and floored it. They peeled out of the drive way. The Simple Plan sticker flew out the window before Jane could catch it.

Well, at least I won't miss my train, she thought, clutching the armrest for dear life.

Click.

Got it. A gray-faced middle-aged man sat in a big tank of a car outside the Ryans' house, snapping a picture of Roxy's VW. Time: 8:02 AM. *Now let's see where she's off to this morning*, he thought. *Dollars to doughnuts it isn't South Side High School.*

The man's name was Max Lomax, and he

was a truant officer. The best darn truant officer on Long Island. He did whatever it took to make sure kids went to school, and he always got his man—or his girl, as the case may be.

Roxanne Ryan was Lomax's public enemy number one. Lots of kids cut school, but she was the big fish. Lomax was determined to catch her.

He started his car and followed her down the street. Something flew out of Roxy's window. Lomax stopped the car, opened the door, and leaned down to pick it up.

Aha! It was a sticker for a band called Simple Plan. *This could be a clue*, Lomax thought. He sped off after Roxy.

You won't get away this time, Roxy Ryan, he thought. *Today you're going down.*

2

Roxy zoomed down a quiet suburban street and hit the brakes when she spotted Justin DeMarco's house.

"Why are we stopping?" Jane asked. "We have twenty-six minutes to get to the train station. I can't be late."

"This will only take a minute," Roxy promised. "I've got to make a pit stop at my manager's."

"You have a manager?" Jane asked.

"Well, I have a Justin," Roxy admitted. Justin was a friend of hers from school and a big fan of her rock band. He was playing the role of manager until the band got big enough to hire a real one. And Roxy hoped that day was coming soon, because Justin wasn't much of an organizer. Maybe today was the day. Maybe she'd meet a record executive at the video shoot and start down the road to fame and fortune!

"I'll be right back," she told Jane. She jumped out of the car and dashed around the side of Justin's house to the backyard and hurried through the gate, closing it behind her. No use knocking on the front door. She knew exactly where to look for Justin on a beautiful day like this—by the pool.

Just as she thought, she found four scruffy guys—her band mates Sam Mahallik, Ryan Greenhut, Matt Fidler, and Dan Collins—hanging around the pool, tunes blasting from the stereo.

Justin came out of the house with a stack of CDs in one hand. He had short hair, stubby legs, and a small potbelly—he already looked like some kind of wheeler-dealer businessman.

"Hey, Roxy—you're off to the city?" Justin asked.

Roxy nodded. "You sure you can't come with me? It doesn't look like you're too busy here."

"Sorry, I can't," Justin said. "My dad's flying in from L.A. today. Got to pick him up at the airport."

"It's cool," Roxy said. "Little early for a

pool party, Justin." It was only 8:15 in the morning.

Justin laughed. "You mean a little late. We've been going since eight last night."

Roxy waved to the rockers slacking off in their lounge chairs. "What's up, guys?"

"Hey, Rox! What's up?" they called back.

Justin handed her the stack of the band's demo CDs. "I burned you thirty copies."

"Cool," Roxy said. She glanced at the cover. It was a picture of her—and her alone—in tight jeans and a black leather jacket, her blond hair blowing back. Wow! She really looked like a rock star! But where was the rest of the band?

"Why is it only me on cover?" she asked Justin. "I'm just the drummer."

"Marketing, baby," Justin replied. "You're the hottest one in the band."

Roxy glanced across the pool at her scraggly band mates with their goofy grins. Sam's black hair stuck up at the back, Matt had dark rings under his brown eyes from staying up all night, Ryan's red T-shirt was dirty and torn at one sleeve, and Dan's denim cut-off shorts hung precariously on his bony, skinny hips. They were kind of cute in a scruffy way, but there wasn't a hottie among them.

That left Roxy. "The hottest one in the band? That's not saying a lot," Roxy said.

"I know." Justin gave her a green laminated pass. "This is an All Access pass that will get you into the shoot. Remember, target the A-and-R guys. We want to get a contract."

The A-and-R guys were the record executives who signed new bands. "How will I spot them?" Roxy asked.

"Middle-aged men," Justin said. "Goatees. Expensive suits. Old-school dance moves."

Someone knocked at the backyard gate.

"Yeah?" Justin called over the tall wooden fence.

"Pool guy!" a voice shouted back.

"Hang on!" Justin said. He turned to Roxy. "Good luck. You can leave through the house if you want."

Roxy stuffed the CDs into her bag and slid open the glass door that led into Justin's house. She paused in the kitchen. Something bothered her. Pool guy? So early in the morning? Something didn't feel right about this.

She glanced through the kitchen window,

which looked out on the narrow yard at the side of the house. She got a glimpse of the "pool guy" waiting by the backyard gate.

That curly black hair and wrinkled gray face looked familiar. Too familiar. Then Roxy realized how she knew him. He wasn't a pool guy! He was Lomax, the truant officer!

I'd better get out of here—fast! Roxy raced out of the house and jumped into the VW.

"What took you so long?" Jane asked.

Roxy dumped her bag into Jane's lap and started the car.

"Nothing," Roxy said. "Let's go."

She slammed her foot on the gas and peeled out of there, tires squealing.

Lomax's palms began to sweat as he waited for Justin to open the gate. Finally the infamous Roxy Ryan was going to be caught. He had followed her to Justin's house and had seen her go through the backyard gate. Yes, she was definitely there.

"Yeah?" Justin said as he opened the gate. He stared at Lomax. "Hey, you're not the pool guy," he said.

Lomax adjusted his aviator sunglasses and shot a glance at Justin's stocky body. "Wow.

Step to the head of the class, stubby. Excuse me." He brushed past Justin and headed toward the four guys lounging by the pool.

"Won't you come in?" Justin snapped sarcastically.

Lomax ignored him. Justin DeMarco was small potatoes. Roxy was the one he wanted. He surveyed the situation at the pool. Four boys in shorts and swim trunks, hanging out in patio chairs. No sign of Roxy—yet.

Lomax flashed his badge at Justin. "Nassau County Department of Truancy," he announced. "Sit over there and put your hands behind your head." He motioned Justin toward an empty lounge chair near the others.

The boys looked confused at the sight of his badge, just as Lomax had hoped. Justin sat down.

"Put your hands up where I can see them!" Lomax ordered. The boys did as they were told. "Too nice a day to spend in the classroom, huh? It's okay—you're all relatively fresh offenders. Small fish in the big pond we call *truancy*. It's not you I'm after, boys. It's the girl, Roxanne Ryan. Where is she?"

"She's not here," Justin said, but Lomax

thought he saw Justin flinch just a little. The liar. She was here somewhere.

"Who do you think you're messing with?" Lomax demanded. "Don't toy with me, because you're in over your head. Now let's try this again. Where's Roxanne Ryan?"

"She just left," Justin said.

Lomax stared at Justin. Justin stared back. He *was* lying, wasn't he? Of course he was.

"Seriously, she just left," one of the messy-haired boys said.

"She's not here, man. Really," another one added.

Lomax's eyes didn't leave Justin's. When it came to a stare-down, Lomax always won. He'd walked right past Roxy's car on his way to the house. She had to be there. These boys weren't going to put anything over on Lomax.

"Okay, fellas," he said. "Have it your way. You're all truant. I'm taking you in."

Lomax had already called his friend, Officer Strauss of the Nassau County Police Department. Strauss should be waiting outside Justin's house with a police van, just in case there was any trouble.

"On your feet," Lomax ordered. "Come

with me boys. If you resist, I'll have you arrested."

"What?" Justin protested.

"Oh, man," Dan groaned.

Lomax led the boys away from the pool, through the gate and around the house to the front yard. Just as he'd thought, Officer Strauss was waiting for them outside his van.

"Got five truants for you," Lomax said.

"You can't do this! My uncle's a lawyer," Justin protested. "You don't have a leg to stand on!"

"I've got two legs and they suit me just fine," Lomax said. "I think you'll be looking at at least five to ten—"

"—days of detention," Officer Strauss finished.

"Book 'em, Danno." Lomax swaggered as he said it.

"Come on, Lomax, give it a rest," Strauss said. "You're a truancy officer, not Dirty Harry. It's this kind of nonsense that's kept you off the police force for the past twelve years."

Lomax winced. Strauss had hit a nerve. More than anything Lomax wanted to be a real police officer.

"That's not true," Lomax said. "We both

know they've kept me off the force because I failed the physical."

"Not to mention the written test and the practical exam," Strauss added.

Lomax grimaced. He didn't like to be reminded of any of this. "I've had just about enough of your lip, Strauss," he snapped. "It just so happens that while you're bringing in the small-time truants here, I'm about to collar Roxanne Ryan."

"So?" Strauss asked.

"So, it's more than any truant officer or cop on the beat can say. She's the most notorious truant in Nassau County since Jim 'Skip' Martin in 1976. This is going to be my big break."

Strauss rolled his eyes.

Lomax glanced at Justin, who'd been watching them the whole time. He wheeled around to face the boy, hoping to catch him off guard. "So I'm asking you one last time—where can I find Roxy Ryan?" he said.

"Dude, you can give me all the detention you want, but if there's one thing I'm not it's a rat," Justin said.

Lomax started to lead him into the back of the van. "'Dear Justin's parents,'" he said, trying to sound like the admissions officer of a college. "'We can't accept your son to our college. Ten days of detention? He must be some kind of juvenile delinquent!'"

"Okay, okay! She's gone to a video shoot in Manhattan!" Justin blurted out.

Sam Mahallik put his arm around Justin and said, "Nice going, rat man."

Lomax grinned. *A video shoot, eh?* He remembered the band sticker that flew out of Roxy's car window. He reached into his pocket and pulled it out. SIMPLE PLAN, it said. He waved it in front of Justin's face.

"Yeah, man, Simple Plan," Justin said. "Where did you get that?"

Aha! That was all Lomax needed to hear. All he had to do now was go back to his office and do a computer search for a Simple Plan video shoot—and he had her.

He rubbed his hands together. *Your simple plan is about to get a bit more complicated, Roxanne Ryan!*

"Nice parking job," Jane said as Roxy maneuvered the VW into the last tiny spot left in the train station parking lot. "See you later."

"Thanks," Roxy said. "Later."

Jane jumped out of the car and hurried to the platform. Roxy headed for the newsstand. Jane knew Roxy was cutting school that day, but she had no idea where she was going or what she was doing, and she didn't have time to worry about it. She planned on using her time on the train to practice her McGill Fellowship speech, and she didn't need Roxy around to distract her.

Jane checked her day planner to make sure her ticket was still safely tucked away inside. Yep, there it was. She'd bought her ticket in advance to save time. It was just the way she did things.

She walked onto a nearly full Manhattan-bound train waiting on the platform. She spotted an empty seat by a window and made her way to it. A man in a suit, an executive type, was sitting in the middle of a three-seat row, paying his bills using an expensive-looking fountain pen to write checks. He was nice-looking, with graying blond hair, maybe forty years old.

He won't bother me while I'm working, Jane thought. "Excuse me," she asked the man. "Is that seat taken?"

The man looked up at her. He seemed a

little annoyed, but what could Jane do? She had to sit somewhere. He picked up his papers from the window seat and let her slip past him.

Jane settled into her seat and started her usual travel routine. She pulled out an antibacterial wipe and cleaned off the armrests. Then she took a plastic neck-support cushion from her bag and began to blow it up. She snapped open a portable lap desk and fanned out her note cards. At last she was ready to work.

She checked her alarm watch. 8:31. Perfect. The train was scheduled to leave at 8:35.

She picked up her note cards. "Good morning, ladies and gentlemen," she whispered to herself. "My name is—"

"Dude looks like a lady!" someone squawked from the aisle in a loud, flat singing voice. Jane was afraid to look, but she couldn't stop her eyes from glancing toward the sound.

Roxy had her headphones on and was singing along with an Aerosmith CD only she could hear. Her arms were loaded with snacks and magazines and she twirled a drumstick as she screeched out the song.

Jane slouched low in her seat, hoping Roxy wouldn't notice her. She'd never get anything done if Roxy sat anywhere near her.

But there was only one empty seat left in the car—the aisle seat in Jane's row, on the other side of the bill-paying executive. Actually the seat wasn't quite empty—the executive had set his pile of bills on it.

Roxy dropped into the seat anyway, right on top of the bills. The executive nudged her. She lifted her butt up, pulled out the pile of papers, and handed them to the executive.

Jane squeezed her eyes shut in frustration. *Why me? Why does Roxy have to pick today, the most important day of my life, to tag along?*

"Uh-uh, no way," Jane said to Roxy. "You cannot sit there. I need quiet. Right now."

"Chill out," Roxy said. "You won't even know I'm here."

"Listen to me," Jane said. "I am *this close* to winning the McGill Fellowship. I've worked my whole life for this."

Out of the corner of her eye Jane thought she saw the executive raise an eyebrow when she mentioned the McGill Fellowship. He was eavesdropping, but what could she do?

"What is this stupid thing anyway?" Roxy asked.

"This *'stupid thing'* is a four-year scholarship to Oxford University," Jane explained.

"Oxford, as in England?" Roxy asked.

Jane rolled her eyes. "No, Oxford as in France."

"Maybe one of you would like to trade seats with me so it would be easier for you to fight," the executive offered.

"NO!" Jane and Roxy answered at once.

The train started moving. Jane stared at her note cards, but she couldn't focus on them. Just being within a few feet of Roxy was distracting. She sighed and put down her cards. "Why are you even here?" she asked Roxy.

"Simple Plan is shooting a video and I'm going to canvas the A-and-R guys," Roxy explained. "Who knows? Maybe we'll get to audition as backup for the tour."

Jane shook her head. A rock video—she should have known. Roxy was living in a dream world. Why couldn't she be more practical or aim for something important, like a college scholarship?

"That's great," Jane said. "You'll need the

experience, because there will be a lot of rock concerts at Sister Mary Margaret's. The convent is practically Madison Square Garden."

Roxy shrugged. "How am I going to get busted? As far as the school knows, I'm home sick with chicken pox."

Jane worried about Roxy. As much as her sister could get on her nerves sometimes, she hated to think of her at a convent school. But one of these days, if she didn't change her ways, Roxy was going to get caught.

3

Ba-ba-bum, ba-ba-ba-bum . . . Roxy tapped out a beat with her drumsticks on the back of the seat in front of her. The woman sitting there turned around and frowned at her. Roxy rolled her eyes and stopped. *Now* what should she do? It was hard for her to sit still.

I'm hungry, Roxy thought. *Maybe some popcorn*. She tried to tear open the bag of cheese popcorn she'd bought at the newsstand, but it wouldn't open. *These stupid bags* . . .

She gave it one last rip. *Poof!* The bag burst open and popcorn spewed all over the car like confetti. Several puffs landed on the executive's suit and plopped into his cup of coffee.

"Oops," Roxy said. Great. Now Mr. Uptight Businessman was going to be even madder at her.

Jane picked some popcorn out of her hair. "Roxanne Ryan, ladies and gentlemen." She started to applaud, but her hand knocked over the executive's coffee cup. Hot coffee poured into his lap.

"Ah! Ah!" The man cried out in pain.

"OhmyGod, ohmyGod!" Jane shrieked. "I'm so sorry. . . ." She grabbed some of the man's papers and tried to clean him off.

The executive fanned his pants. "Hot stuff, hot stuff . . ."

At least this disaster is Jane's fault for once, Roxy thought. *I know how to fix this.* She grabbed her large, icy soda and dumped it into the executive's lap.

"What the heck is wrong with you?" he shouted. He leaped to his feet, grabbed his things and stormed out of the car.

"I just saved you from scalding hot coffee and disfiguring blisters!" Roxy yelled after him. Didn't he get it? To stop a burn you apply ice. Any doctor's daughter knew that. "You should be thanking me!" she added. She turned to Jane, who was staring at her with one eyebrow raised in severe disapproval—a look Roxy knew only too well. "I was just trying to help."

"That's what you always say," Jane said.

Roxy crossed her arms and slumped in her seat. Why couldn't Jane lighten up a little? She always acted as if Roxy was bothering her. As if she didn't want Roxy around.

It hadn't always been that way. The sisters were superclose when they were little. Sure, they were always different from each other, but that was the fun of it. Then, after their mother died, Jane turned into a total control freak.

"Tickets please. Tickets please."

Roxy looked up and spotted the train conductor working his way toward her through the car. *Uh-oh, here comes the man*, she thought.

Roxy checked her wallet—empty. She'd blown all her money at the newsstand on magazines and snacks. She'd forgotten she'd need a train ticket. *I should have driven into the city*, she thought. But she wasn't sure the VW would make it that far, and parking in Manhattan was murder.

"Tickets please." The conductor was getting closer.

"I suppose you need to borrow some money?" Jane asked.

"I can manage on my own." Roxy refused

to give Jane the satisfaction of bailing her out once again. She got up and slinked down the aisle, heading for the rest room at the back of the car. There had to be a way around this ticket thing.

Oof! A big, burly Asian man bumped into her in the aisle. Roxy waited for him to excuse himself, but he said nothing.

"Excuse you," Roxy cracked.

He shot her an evil look and hurried past her.

"Rude," Roxy said to herself. She pushed on the rest room door, but it didn't open. She knocked. "Anybody in there?" No one answered.

She had to hurry. The conductor was almost at the end of the car! She jiggled the handle. *It must be stuck*, she thought. Then she took a step back and kicked the door— hard. It flew open and smacked against something—or someone.

"Ow!" the person cried. It was the executive!

Oh, no, not again! Roxy thought. The man was standing at the sink in his smiley-face boxer shorts, trying to wash the coffee and soda stains out of his pants. He glared at her with one red, swollen eye. His nose was red too. The door must have hit him in the face!

This guy is going to hate me for life! Roxy thought. "I'm so sorry," she said to him. "Your nose—" She reached out to help.

He backed away from her. "Don't touch me! Don't. Touch. Me. Just leave me alone. Forever!"

He grabbed his stuff and stormed out of the rest room in his boxers.

"Can I get you some ice?" Roxy asked.

"LEAVE ME ALONE!" he shouted.

Poor guy, Roxy thought, slipping into the bathroom. She leaned against the door and heard a knock. *Must be that executive dude again*, Roxy thought. She opened the door. "I said I was sorry. . . ." she began.

But it wasn't the executive. It was the conductor. "Ticket?"

Okay, I messed that up big-time, Roxy thought. *But I can still squirm out of it somehow. I'll turn on the charm.*

"Hey, why don't we just bypass the whole 'give me your ticket' deal and let the rules slide for a change," she suggested, smiling sweetly at the conductor. She held out her hand so he could slap her five. "My mannnn . . ."

It didn't work. The conductor dragged her out of the bathroom. The train squealed to a stop at the next station. He marched her to an open door and threw her off the train!

She landed on her butt on the platform, her drumsticks bouncing beside her. "That was so uncool!" Roxy yelled.

She caught Jane watching through the window. Jane waved and smiled.

Hey, yourself, Roxy thought, waving back. She stood up and dusted herself off. *See, Jane? Being me isn't all fun and games. But it's not too bad either,* she added to herself, remembering the video shoot. *All I have to do is find another way to get into the city. No problem!*

Poor Rox, Jane thought. *She should really be more organized.* Well, Jane couldn't help her now. Besides, her McGill Fellowship speech was a lot more important than Roxy's silly video shoot.

Jane reached back to adjust her neck-support pillow, but it got caught on her hair clip. Her neat French twist fell apart, and her wavy blond hair tumbled down around her shoulders.

"Oh, no," Jane muttered to herself, trying

to put her hair back up. "I forgot to bring my portable mirror."

The conductor stopped and stared at Jane as she fussed with her hair. He blinked. Jane smiled at him, but he kept staring at her as if he couldn't believe his eyes.

"Do you think a new hairdo is going to fool me?" the conductor demanded.

"Excuse me?" Jane said.

The conductor grabbed her by the arm and started to pull her out of her seat. "No ticket, no ride," he said.

Oh, no! He thought she was Roxy! Jane dug through her day planner, searching for her ticket. She knew it was in there somewhere.

"Wait! I have a ticket," she said. "If you'll just give me a minute—"

"Sure, sure," the conductor said. "Let's go." He pulled Jane into the aisle. She scrambled to gather her things.

"But my ticket's right here!" She held up her day planner. "That was my twin sister you just threw off the train!"

"The old twin-sister scam. Do I look that stupid to you?" the conductor asked, dragging her to the door.

Jane stared at his blank face. As a matter

of fact, he *did* look kind of stupid. "I assume that's a rhetorical question," she said.

"Very funny," the conductor said. He pulled her down the aisle and escorted her toward the open doors.

This is just great, Jane thought. She felt like a criminal and avoided the stares of the other passengers. *Thanks a lot, Roxy.*

A crowd of passengers was pushing to board the train as Jane tried to step off. Something tugged on her skirt. "Ow!" She stopped. Her skirt was caught on a bicycle chain! *Great. What else could go wrong?* she wondered, annoyed.

Then Jane looked up at the bike's owner and her irritation melted away. He was a clean-cut college guy with neat brown hair and soft brown eyes. He wore a fleece pull-over and khakis.

Hmm, Jane thought, gazing at him. *Cute.*

"Oh, man, I'm sorry," the guy said. "Here, give me a sec." He struggled to free her skirt from the chain, but it was really jammed.

"God, you're cute," Jane said. *What did I just do?* she thought with a jolt. "Did I just say that out loud?"

He smiled, and their eyes met. She blushed.

He looked down at her skirt again, trying to unhook it. "I think you're really stuck," he said.

"Let me try." Jane reached down and tugged on the skirt. Together they gave one big yank. *Rrriiiip!* Both Jane and the guy fell onto the platform.

Jane looked down at her skirt. At least she was free from the bike chain, but her skirt was slit all the way up the side.

The bike guy got to his feet and looked down at Jane's legs. "Nice," he said, helping her up.

Jane smiled.

"All aboard!" the conductor shouted. "Except for *you*," he warned Jane.

The bike guy stepped back onto the train, and the doors closed.

Jane took one last look at the cute boy as the train pulled out of the station. He waved to her and watched her until she couldn't see him any longer. She sighed. He was gone forever. But Jane felt as if something important had just happened to her. She couldn't explain it or put it into words, which was unusual for her. Such a brief encounter, but something about that guy felt *right* to her.

Roxy sauntered over and stared at Jane's

torn skirt. "The shredded look is so fifteen minutes ago."

Jane was not in the mood for her sister's jokes. She had to find another train and get on it. And she had to find a way to fix her torn skirt before her speech. And Roxy couldn't help her with either of those things. As far as she was concerned, Roxy couldn't help her with much of anything.

"Stay away from me," Jane warned.

"Whatever you say." Roxy walked away and left Jane standing on the platform.

Jane's alarm watch beeped. *That means I'm supposed to do something or remember something*, Jane thought. *But what?*

Oh, well. She'd figure it out later. Right now she had to get on another train to the city—fast. She marched up to the ticket window. "One way to Penn Station, please," Jane said to the clerk. She pulled a Long Island Railroad schedule out of her day planner. She'd highlighted the next train, in case disaster struck and she missed the 8:35. Well, now disaster had struck. But if she caught the 9:40 she'd be okay.

"You realize the next train doesn't leave for three hours," the ticket clerk said.

"What?" Jane waved her schedule at the clerk. "According to this schedule, there should be another train in forty-three minutes."

"Not today there isn't," the clerk said. "Track construction. Next train to New York is in three hours."

"That's not possible," Jane said. "There must be another train!"

"Of course, how could I have forgotten?" the clerk said with a sneer. "The magic leprechaun train! It leaves for New York whenever you want it to . . . powered by your imagination."

"You don't understand," Jane said. "I've got to go into the city now. On a real train, not a leprechaun train!"

"Next!" the ticket clerk called.

What am I going to do? Jane thought. Was everybody conspiring against her that day? Why did things keep going wrong?

I've got to get into the city somehow—but how?

4

Maybe I can get a cab, Roxy thought, heading for a taxi stand. *Of course, I have no money to pay the fare, but I'll figure it out.*

There was one cab at the taxi stand, four commuters angrily fighting over it, and no other cabs in sight. *Guess I'll have to find another way*, Roxy thought. Then she noticed a big, beefy Asian guy walking down the platform. Wasn't that the rude man who'd bumped into her on the train?

There's Chang, right on schedule, Bennie Bang thought, watching that same beefy Asian guy get off the train and head down the platform. *So far, so good.*

Wearing his black chauffeur's uniform and cap, Bennie stood in front of a shiny black stretch limousine waiting to meet

Chang. This was a very important drop-off. Chang was walking casually toward Bennie, about to slip him a microchip. A valuable microchip. If Bennie didn't get the chip to his boss that afternoon, he'd be dead meat.

Chang nodded at Bennie and patted his jacket pocket. He had the chip all right. All Bennie had to do was take it.

He started toward Chang, then stopped. Trouble. Two men in dark suits and dark glasses moved swiftly toward Chang. The FBI! They were on to him!

Bennie backed up to his limo. He didn't want the Feds to catch him. *Dump the chip somewhere*, he silently begged Chang. Without the chip, the FBI wouldn't have any evidence.

As the agents moved in, Chang passed a blond teenage girl dressed in torn jeans, carrying a leather shoulder bag and a pair of drumsticks. Bennie watched as Chang bumped into her and slipped the microchip into her bag. Then Chang disappeared into the crowd.

Good going, Chang, Bennie thought. Now all he had to do was get the chip off the girl . . . and that would be easy.

• • •

"There you are." A large, burly bald man in a chauffeur's outfit approached Roxy. He was built like a bodyguard but had the chubby cheeks of a man who ate a lot of greasy food. He stood in front of a long black limo and wore a nametag that read BENNIE.

If only Roxy could take that limo to the video shoot—arrive in style. Then the A-and-R guys would really notice her. "Here I am," Roxy replied, wondering what he wanted.

"How about I give you a ride?" the chauffeur offered.

"No," Roxy said. She didn't have any cash for the train. How was she supposed to pay for a limo?

"How about I give you a *free* ride?" Bennie offered again.

"Sorry, but I don't take rides from strangers," Roxy said, trying to decide if this guy was a creep or not.

"I was supposed to pick up a business client, but he didn't show up," Bennie said. "So I have to drive my limo back into the city empty. Might as well take a passenger, I thought. Help someone out. I see people fighting over the last taxi over there."

Roxy checked out the limo and Bennie. He *seemed* legit. And she *did* need a ride—badly—and so did Jane.

"All right," she agreed. "I'm going to midtown Manhattan. Just wait a second and I'll be right back." She hurried to the ticket window, where Jane was still arguing with the clerk. She tapped on Jane's shoulder. "Jane—"

Jane wouldn't look at her. "Is someone talking?" Jane asked no one in particular. "I don't hear anyone."

"Just wanted you to know I might be able to squeeze you into my limo if you're still looking for a ride," Roxy said.

"No way," Jane said.

Why did Jane have to be so stubborn? Roxy was only trying to help. "Fine. Good luck with your presentation." Roxy walked away and flashed Bennie a smile. He opened the back door for her.

She'll change her mind when she sees me getting into this limo, Roxy thought.

Bennie reached for her bag. "I'll take that," he said.

Roxy clutched the bag tightly. She had to hang on to her precious CDs. "That won't be necessary."

"But I insist," Bennie said in a sweet voice. He grabbed the bag.

Roxy grabbed it back. "But *I* insist."

"Give me the bag," Bennie said, tugging on it.

Roxy smiled. "Not on your life." She snatched the bag away and climbed into the back seat of the limo. No way was Bigfoot getting her bag.

"Wait for me!" Jane called, rushing over.

Ha! I knew she'd change her mind, Roxy thought. "That's my personal assistant," she told Bennie. "I'd be lost without her."

Bennie held the door open for Jane. "My name is Bennie. Are you and her going to the same place?"

"You mean you and *she*," Jane corrected him. "You see, 'she' is the subject of the sentence, not the object, so—"

This was no time for Miss Grammar. "Just get in," Roxy said. She reached out and yanked Jane into the car. Bennie closed the door. In a few seconds the car started and they were on their way.

"Cool, isn't it?" Roxy said. "Check this out." She fiddled with some buttons on an armrest panel. With a hum, the glass partition between the girls and the driver's seat opened.

"How's it going?" Roxy asked Bennie. She pressed the button again, and the partition closed. "I could get used to this." Lots of legroom, plenty of gadgets to play with . . . this was the way to travel. She started to press the partition button again, but Jane grabbed her hand.

"Enough," Jane said.

She looks nervous, Roxy thought. "Relax, Jane. Everything's going to be okay now. We're on our way into the city, we've got a smooth, comfortable ride. . . . What's to worry about?"

Jane took some instant hand sanitizer from her bag and rubbed it onto her hands. She did that a lot when she was nervous.

Roxy fooled with the control panel some more. "Want some moon roof?"

"No thanks," Jane said.

"Tunes?"

"I'm fine."

"Butt heat?" Roxy offered, her finger hovering over the seat warmer button.

"Roxy, attempt to be cool," Jane said. "I'm going to study my speech."

Roxy slumped in her seat while Jane took out her note cards. *Always with the note cards and the nerd book*, Roxy thought. She pressed the seat warmer button. *Maybe some butt heat will relax her.*

In the front seat, Bennie called Ma Bang's Nail Parlor on his cell phone.

"Where are you?" Ma demanded in Chinese. "You said you'd be here by nine. That was twenty minutes ago."

"Sorry, Ma," Bennie said. Ma was his adoptive mother and his boss. She kind of scared him. "I've got the chip with me." It was in the car, at least. He'd get it from the girl as soon as they got into Manhattan. "I'll be there soon."

"Whatever, Bennie," Ma said. "Just get me that chip."

Roxy stared out the window as the limo crossed the Manhattan Bridge. New York City sparkled in the morning sun. It was a beautiful day for a video shoot.

"Oh my God," Jane moaned. She sweated and squirmed in her seat. "I think I'm getting sick. I've got a fever!"

Roxy felt Jane's forehead. It was a little warm but not exactly burning up. Then she remembered the seat warmer. That must be what was making Jane feel hot.

"No, do you really think you're getting sick?" Roxy asked.

Jane nodded. "This is great. I'm getting sick right before the most important moment of my life."

"You're not getting sick," Roxy said. "It's all in your head."

"You think so?" Jane asked.

"Trust me," Roxy said. She casually moved her hand over to the control panel, hoping Jane wouldn't notice. Then she quickly flicked the seat warmer button off. "You'll be fine before you know it."

She turned back to the window. Poor Jane. She took everything too hard. She needed to learn to just relax and enjoy the ride.

The car drove across Canal Street and then headed south into Chinatown.

Shouldn't we be going uptown? Roxy wondered. She lowered the glass partition and called out to Bennie. "Hey, bud, are you lost? This doesn't look right."

Click. The doors suddenly locked. What was going on?

"Ancient Chinese proverb," Bennie said. "'Never take rides from strangers.'"

The glass partition went back up. Roxy tried her door. It wouldn't open and she couldn't budge the lock! She glanced at Jane, who was really sweating now.

"What's going on?" Jane asked.

Roxy didn't want to answer. This looked bad—really bad.

Jane frantically tore at the door locks, trying to open them.

Roxy tried to put the partition down, but it wouldn't move. She banged on the glass. "Let us out of here, Bennie, or you're in big trouble!"

Bennie turned his head and gave them an evil grin through the glass. That was when Roxy knew it was hopeless. He wasn't letting them go anywhere!

5

"This can't be good," Jane said. "We're trapped!" She tried to open a window, but it wouldn't roll down. Then she flailed her arms, pounding on the windows. "Help!"

"Help!" Roxy shouted, banging on the windows too.

"What are we going to do?" Jane asked.

Roxy looked at the roof of the car. She pressed a button on the control panel. The moon roof slid open.

"He forgot to lock it!" Jane said. "Roxy, you're a genius!"

The girls scrambled out of the car through the moon roof. They balanced on top of the limo and looked around.

"Now what?" Jane asked. The car stopped. She gripped the top to keep from tumbling off.

The driver's door opened. Bennie was getting out!

"What should we do?" Jane whispered. "Where should we go?" But there was no time to go anywhere. Bennie spotted them huddled on the roof.

"There you are!" he shouted.

Jane and Roxy screamed. They slid off the other side of the car and ran down the street.

Jane glanced back. "He's chasing us!" she cried.

Roxy pointed to a subway station entrance. "That way!"

They scurried down the stairs into the subway. An old lady swiped her fare card and started to walk through a turnstile. No time to buy a Metrocard. Jane pressed herself against the woman's back. Roxy pressed against Jane. Together they all pressed through the turnstile, three for the price of one.

Bennie ran to a revolving gate entrance and slammed all his weight against it. But someone was coming out the other way and pressed back.

"He's stuck for now," Jane said. "Let's go!"

They ran the length of the platform to

another flight of stairs, dashed down the steps two at a time and found themselves on another empty subway platform.

Jane looked around. No sign of Bennie. No sign of anyone.

"I think we lost him," Roxy said. "Do you think we lost him?"

Jane turned around, backed up past a thick pillar—and bumped right into Bennie. "Ahhh!" she screamed.

A subway train pulled in, brakes squealing. Bennie stood between the girls and the train. The doors opened and an old man with a cane wobbled out.

They had nowhere to run. Behind them was a brick wall. To their right, the same. To their left, the train. In front of them, Bennie.

"Give me the bag!" Bennie yelled in Chinese.

"Leave us alone!" Jane shouted back in Chinese. *Good thing I took that Chinese class last year,* she thought.

Bennie looked startled. So did her sister.

"What's going on?" Roxy asked her. "You speak Chinese?"

"Don't be an idiot," Bennie said, still in Chinese. "You're making me very mad."

"Calling you an idiot would be an insult to idiots," Jane shot back.

Bennie's face turned red and he roared with rage.

Whoops, Jane thought. *Guess I just made him even madder.*

"Way to go, United Nations," Roxy snapped.

Bennie snatched the old man's cane away from him and swung it at the girls.

"Hold this." Roxy tossed her bag to Jane and struck a martial arts pose. Jane stepped back as Roxy faced off with Bennie. "Bring it!" Roxy said.

Bennie charged Roxy. With a one-two punch Roxy kicked him in the head. Then, with a running leap, she kicked him right into the subway car. *Dingdong!* The bells sounded and the doors closed him in.

"Nice one!" Jane cheered. "I didn't know you knew karate."

"There's a lot about me you don't know," Roxy said.

The train pulled away. Bennie raged in the car, banging on the doors. Jane and Roxy blew kisses at him and waved.

"Safe trip!" Jane called after him.

"*Arrivederci!*" Roxy said.

Jane took a deep breath and started toward the exit.

"So when did you learn Chinese?" Roxy asked.

"There's a lot about me *you* don't know," Jane replied. And it was true, Jane realized. She felt a twinge of sadness.

They walked up the subway stairs and came out onto the street, blinking in the bright sunshine. They were about a block from City Hall, way downtown, far from Columbia University, which was all the way uptown on West 116th Street.

"Well, that was exciting," Roxy said.

"Exciting?" Jane cried. *How could Roxy take something so serious so lightly!* "Almost getting killed by a homicidal maniac is not my definition of *exciting.*" Then one of Jane's pointy heels got caught in a crack in the sidewalk. She lost her balance and tumbled to the ground. "Ow!" She sat up, dazed.

Roxy grinned at her from above. "That was more like my definition of *clumsy.*"

"You're hilarious." Jane pulled herself to her feet and picked up one of her pumps. The heel had fallen off and the shoe was ruined. "These were my best heels."

"Let me see the other one," Roxy said.

Jane took off her good shoe and handed it to Roxy. What did she want it for?

Roxy took the shoe, smacked it against a garbage can until the heel fell off, and gave it back to Jane. "Now they're your best flats," she said.

"Thanks a ton," Jane snapped, putting on her flat, broken shoes. Why was Roxy's idea of helpful somehow never quite right? "Come on, maybe we can catch a taxi uptown."

They passed a homeless man sitting against a wall next to an empty liquor bottle, sipping a bright purple slushie through a straw. "Can either of you nice young ladies spare some change?" he asked.

Roxy stopped and dug into her jeans pocket. Jane stared at her. What was she doing now?

Roxy pulled a crumpled dollar bill out of her pocket. "Here." She started to hand it to the homeless guy, who managed to pinch it between his fingers before Jane reached out and tried to grab it herself. All three of them were holding on to the bill.

"I thought you didn't have any money," Jane said.

"It's my emergency single," Roxy explained. "Let it go."

"You're only feeding this poor man's disease," Jane said. "Why don't you use it to buy him a healthy snack?"

Everyone tugged on the bill, but Jane tugged the hardest and snatched it away. Her hand knocked against the guy's slushie cup and sent it flying. Roxy ducked, but Jane didn't have time. She watched the neon-purple goo sail toward her as if in slow motion.

Noooooo! Jane wanted to scream, but she didn't have time to open her mouth.

Splat! The purple slush splashed her from head to toe. It stained her suit and worst of all, her once spotless white blouse. Jane wanted to cry.

Roxy sniffed Jane's hair. "Whoa, that's not just a grape slushie."

"Ugh!" Jane screamed. How could she give her speech covered in grape slushie? Grape slushie that stank of whiskey!

Roxy pulled a bandanna from her bag and dabbed at Jane's top.

Jane knew it wouldn't do any good. "I'm

not going to cry," she said bravely, but it was very hard.

"Please don't freak," Roxy said. "It's going to be fine. You can wear my clothes to the presentation."

Roxy's clothes? Ripped jeans and a vintage rock T-shirt? That wouldn't make a very good impression on the panel. Still, it was better than looking as if she hadn't bothered to shower—or worse yet, showered in purple dye #2.

"Thanks, Roxy—" Jane began. A truck rumbled past, splashing through a huge, muddy puddle in the street. "Ahhh!" She was soaked in dirty water—and so was Roxy. Now Roxy's clothes were ruined too! Could this day get any worse?

"Then again . . ." Roxy squeezed the bottom of her stained T-shirt, wringing muddy water from it. She tied it in a knot at her waist.

Jane checked her watch. 10:22! How did it get so late? "Terrific," she fumed. "Let's find a bathroom somewhere. I have to pee, and maybe I can clean myself up enough to look presentable."

They crossed the street and went inside

the first deli they saw. There were no other shops or restaurants on the block.

It wasn't the cleanest place Jane had ever seen—the floor was dirty, and most of the food on the shelves looked dusty and old. But if it had a bathroom, it would have to do.

"May I use your bathroom please?" Jane asked the stone-faced man behind the counter.

The man folded his arms across his chest and glared at her. "The bathroom is for customers only."

Jane sighed and looked around. There wasn't a single thing in the deli she wanted to buy. Roxy helped her out by picking up a piece of bubble gum and slapping it onto the counter.

The clerk frowned. "Down the aisle to the left," he grumbled.

Jane shuffled down the aisle in her heel-less shoes. She pushed open a grimy door with a broken lock. Ew! The smell was rank! But she had to pee badly. She held her breath and stepped inside.

The toilet loomed before her like the mouth of Hell. This was absolutely the grossest bathroom she had ever seen.

Maybe I should wait, she thought. But she

might have to walk for blocks before she found another place that would let her use the bathroom. At least there was toilet paper. She spooled off an armful and covered the toilet seat with five layers of it. *Okay*, she told herself. *Pee really quickly and get out of here.*

Every muscle tense, she carefully sat down on the seat. *Crash!* The seat collapsed—and Jane fell in!

"Aauugh!" she shrieked. She hauled herself out of the toilet, turned on the sink, and tried to wash herself off as well as she could.

It was hopeless. She couldn't stand the stench for another second. She marched out of the bathroom and down the aisle to the counter. Roxy had piled all kinds of candy, snacks, and junk on the counter and was munching on a bag of Doritos. Leave it to Roxy. The clerk was ringing it all up.

"That comes to $64.23," the clerk said. "Cash or charge?"

Roxy stared at Jane. "What did you do, fall in?" Roxy asked.

Jane sneered and walked out.

"Hey, wait!" Roxy called after her. "I need to borrow some cash!"

Cash. The word triggered something in

Jane's mind. Something was missing—something important. Where she kept her cash . . .

Her day planner!

Jane screamed.

"All right, I'm sorry!" Roxy said. "I'll stop borrowing money!"

"No—my planner!" Jane wailed. It had everything in it: her money, her credit card, and, most important of all, her speech! "I must have left it in the limo!"

6

"This is all your fault," Jane grumbled at Roxy as she stalked up the street. She had to get her day planner back, but how? Even if she somehow found the limo among the millions of cars in New York City, she didn't want to run into Bennie again. But she needed that speech! It was worth risking her life for.

"How is it my fault you left your nerd book in the limo?" Roxy demanded.

"It's your fault I was even *in* a limo," Jane shot back. "And without that day planner, I can't function. I mean, I can't even come up with a reason to keep on living."

She stopped and tried to think of one. Nothing was coming to her.

Roxy waited.

"Still trying . . ." Jane said, beginning to hyperventilate. "Still trying . . ."

"Deep breath," Roxy coached. "You need to relax."

"Relax?" Jane cried. "How am I supposed to relax? My relaxation tips are in my *day planner*!"

Beep-beep! Jane's watch alarm went off. She stared at her watch, totally stressed. "I don't even know what this reminder is for!" she shouted. Her breath came fast and shallow. "I'm having a heart attack!"

Whap! Jane felt a bracing slap across her face. What was that for?

"Snap out of it!" Roxy said.

"Don't hit me," Jane said.

"Look, you don't have to give your speech until three. That gives you . . ." She grabbed Jane's wrist and read her watch. "Four and a half hours."

Four and a half hours! Roxy made it sound as if that was a lot of time!

"Roxy, spontaneity doesn't just happen," Jane said. "I need to get there and rehearse. And now look at me. Where am I supposed to clean myself up?"

Roxy got that look on her face—a goofy grin, eyes darting from side to side—that meant she had a nutty idea. Jane didn't like to see that look. Roxy's ideas had a way of going terribly, terribly wrong. On the other hand, what *else* could possibly go wrong that day? Jane was sure that every bad thing in the universe must have happened to her by now.

"I've got a plan," Roxy said. She grabbed Jane by the arm and led her up the street. They crossed into a different neighborhood, a fancier one, with shiny glass shop windows and glittering office towers.

Roxy led Jane to a sleek building guarded by a doorman—the Fairmont Hotel. Jane hung back. How could they go into a fancy place like this looking as if they'd just been mud wrestling?

"Oh, no," she said to Roxy, "I'm not going in there."

Roxy ignored her and dragged her up to the doorman.

"Checking in, ladies?" the doorman asked. Jane was amazed he didn't take one look at them and send them away.

But Roxy knew exactly what to do. "We're with the band."

Jane couldn't help but admire her coolness, but she still didn't get what her sister had in mind. She let Roxy pull her inside.

Okay, so we're in a hotel, Jane thought. *Now what?*

"How could you let them go?" Ma Bang demanded.

Bennie sat across from Ma in her dingy nail salon. Ma was an old Chinese lady who had adopted Bennie as a child. He was very big as a youngster, so Ma thought he'd be useful in her criminal activities. When he was old enough, she made him a member of her gang. Unfortunately, Bennie wasn't so bright. No matter how hard he tried, he was always messing up and disappointing Ma.

"They're smart girls," Bennie explained. "One even speaks Chinese."

Bennie had driven around the neighborhood in his limo, searching for those two blond girls, but they lost him. And now Ma was furious. As usual.

"I don't care if she speaks Hungarian!" Ma shouted. "I want that chip!"

"What's so important about that stupid chip anyway?" Bennie asked.

"That 'stupid chip' contains millions of dollars in pirated music," Ma explained impatiently.

"I still don't understand," Bennie said.

Ma sighed, and Bennie felt stupid for the millionth time that day. "We send the chip to Hong Kong. They transfer the music from the chip to compact disks. Then they sell the pirated CDs and we make millions!"

"Oh." Bennie stood and bowed. "I will get the chip back and bring honor to the family."

"You do that, number one adopted son," Ma snapped.

Bennie went outside to his limo. What could he do? He had no choice but to drive around town, hoping he'd get lucky and spot those girls.

He opened the front door to the limo, but something in the back seat caught his eye. He opened the back door and there it was—the answer to his prayers. An appointment book, filled with addresses, phone numbers, and plans for the day. Otherwise known as a day planner.

Bennie picked up the book and smiled. For once something was going his way. This little book would tell him everything he needed to know.

● ● ●

Jane followed Roxy onto the hotel elevator. Roxy pressed a random button and they rode up in silence.

"Where are we going?" she finally asked.

"You'll see," Roxy answered.

Ding! The elevator doors opened. Roxy pulled Jane off. They were standing in a hallway lined with numbered doors.

"See? I told you my plan would work," Roxy said.

"What plan?" Jane asked. "We're in a hotel hallway."

Jane heard the click of a door being unlocked a few yards away.

"O ye of little faith," Roxy said. She pulled Jane toward the sound. A door opened and an elegant, middle-aged woman stepped out, cell phone glued to her ear. She was tall and thin with short brown hair and dressed in a neat gray suit. Behind her, the door to her room slowly began to ease shut.

She looks familiar, Jane thought as the woman passed her. *Where have I seen her before?*

The woman barely glanced at Jane as she headed for the elevator. She threw her a fake smile and kept talking on her phone.

"No, I'd love to, but I'm supposed to present an award this afternoon," the woman said over the phone.

The elevator doors opened and the woman got on. As the doors closed and the woman disappeared, Roxy whispered, "Now!"

Jane stared as Roxy dashed down the hall toward the woman's room and dove for the door. She jammed a drumstick into the opening just as the door was about to close.

Jane was horrified. "This is your plan?"

Roxy pushed open the door. "What's the problem? Everything's working out great."

"Breaking into a hotel room is exactly how President Nixon went down!" Jane protested. "I am not going in there! I'm not going in there! I'm not going in there!"

Roxy turned Jane's face toward a mirror in the hall. Jane shrieked in terror. Who was that? Scraggly blond hair shooting out at all angles, purple and brown glop covering her face . . . Oh my God, it was her! Jane Ryan!

"Coming?" Roxy asked, stepping into the room.

Jane had no strength left to resist. She followed her in.

"Mmm, food," Roxy said, pointing to a

room service tray covered with leftover breakfast.

Roxy rummaged through the food while Jane took in the room. It was a suite, very expensive, with a bedroom, a sitting room, and a large bathroom. On the desk stood a framed photo. Jane picked it up. It showed the woman who had just left standing next to President Bush. Something clicked.

"Oh my God," Jane said. "I know whose room this is. I know who that woman was! It's Senator Lipton! Anne Baxter Lipton!" A surge of fear ran through her. She jumped up and down nervously. "We've broken into a senator's room! This is a major felony!" She stopped jumping and held her stomach. She had to pee again! "All this anxiety put a strain on my bladder," she said.

"Just get in there and change, will you?" Roxy said, pointing to the bathroom.

Jane staggered to the bathroom. At least this one was guaranteed to be cleaner than the last one she saw.

She threw open the door. There sat a tiny, ugly, beige-colored creature with big pointy ears. Jane shrieked. A monster!

"Oh my God!" she cried. "It's a—"

"Dog," Roxy finished, coming up behind her. "I think. Here, boy."

A dog? Could that weird-looking little thing really be a dog?

The dog raced to Roxy. Jane went into the bathroom and started to take off her wet clothes. Suddenly she heard a panting noise behind her. She turned around. The dog was back, staring at her.

Jane started to shake. She hated dogs, big, medium, or small. But tiny, ugly ones like this made her particularly nervous.

"Go away," Jane ordered. The dog just tilted his head and looked at her. "I mean it! Make tracks."

The dog sat down. He wouldn't take his eyes off her. It gave her the creeps!

"Roxxyy!" Jane called. "Come in here!"

Roxy entered the bathroom wearing a short hotel robe. She'd already ditched her muddy clothes. "What's the matter?"

"I can't change with him watching me," Jane said.

Roxy rolled her eyes. "You get stage fright from a dog?"

"You know I hate dogs," Jane said. "Especially small beady-eyed ones like this."

Jane's cell phone buzzed in her jacket pocket. "What now?" she grumbled. "Jane Ryan speaking."

A low voice said, "I have your date book."

What? It was Bennie! That sicko limo driver! Jane covered the phone with her hand. "It's the psycho!" she told Roxy. "He has my day planner. What should I do?"

"I'll talk to him," Roxy said.

"Nicely," Jane reminded her.

Roxy nodded and took the phone. "Listen, you—" she said angrily.

Jane snatched the phone back. That was no way to talk to a psycho—it might set him off! "Look, you can keep the money and the credit card," she told Bennie, "but please don't hurt the Rolodex. Or my speech!"

"Shut up," Bennie said.

"Good idea," Jane said, shaking. This was life or death. A psychopath had her day planner! She might never see it again!

"You took my chip!" Bennie growled.

Chip? Jane didn't know what he was talking about. She turned to Roxy. "Did you take the man's chips?"

"No," Roxy said.

"She says she didn't eat your chips," Jane

told Bennie. What was the big deal anyway?

"Not my chips, my *chip*," Bennie corrected her. "My computer chip."

"Roxy, go check your bag for a computer chip," Jane said.

Roxy grabbed the phone out of her hand. "Listen, freak show, my sister's going to combust if she doesn't get her nerd book back. So meet us outside the Plaza Hotel in thirty minutes. You provide the book, we'll bring the chips."

She clicked off and tossed the phone to Jane. Jane caught it, hardly knowing what she was doing. How could Roxy talk to a psycho that way? Wasn't she ever afraid?

Jane needs to toughen up, Roxy thought. She left Jane in the bathroom to shower and settled on the bed in her hotel robe. She dumped the contents of her bag onto the bed and sifted through the pile, looking for a microchip, even though she wasn't sure what a microchip looked like. The ugly dog sat beside her on the bed, watching.

A small, thin envelope fell out of the outer pocket of her bag. Roxy definitely didn't recognize it. She opened it. Inside was a tiny piece of metal. That must be it. "Found it!" she called out to Jane.

The bedroom door opened and a guy walked in. "Uh—hey," he said.

Yikes! Roxy was so startled she fell off the bed. Why hadn't she heard this guy come in? The noise from the shower must have muffled the sound of the door.

She sat up, dropped the microchip onto the room service tray next to some leftover rolls, and checked out the guy. He looked about twenty, tall and slim, with straight dark hair falling into his eyes, and he was wearing cool, expensive-looking dark pants and a crisp, white shirt. Not bad. Not bad at all.

"Hey, yourself," Roxy said, getting to her feet.

"You with housekeeping or something?" the guy asked.

"Do I look like I'm with housekeeping?" Roxy shot back. *I mean, come on,* she thought.

"Only in my fantasies," the guy replied.

Hmm, a flirt. Roxy was glad he was the one who'd caught them. She liked him much better than that sour-faced senator.

Jane stepped out of the bathroom, wrapped in a towel. She was too busy drying her hair to notice that they had company. Roxy smiled. Jane was in for a shock.

"Well, here's something you don't see every day," the guy said.

Jane's head jerked up. "Oh! Sorry! We were just leaving!" She spun around and hurried back into the bathroom to get dressed.

Always a nervous wreck, Roxy thought. *Didn't she know a good thing when she saw it?* "I'm Roxy, and that's my sister, Jane," Roxy said.

"I'm Trey," the guy said. "Nice of you to drop in."

Roxy shrugged. "Hey, we were in the neighborhood."

The dog jumped up onto the room service tray and started nosing around the food.

"So what brings you to the city?" Roxy asked Trey.

"Just enjoying the sights," he replied, stepping closer to her. "Look, I like a Doublemint party as much as the next guy, but there's going to be a five-alarm fire if my mom finds you."

Right. Senator Lipton was his mom.

Jane came back into the bedroom, still wrapped in the towel. "Let me explain. You see, this psycho stole my day planner, which has my entire life in it. So we've got to meet him and give him back his computer chip."

Trey nodded, but Roxy thought he looked confused. Understandable. Jane wasn't exactly making sense.

"Hotel break-in?" he said. "Psycho? Computer chip? Sounds logical to me."

"Thank you," Jane said.

Huh? Roxy thought. *So he's just going along with whatever we say. I like that.* She glanced at the dog, who was chewing on a piece of bread. Wait a second . . . *the microchip!*

Roxy jumped and scanned the tray. "The chip! Where's the chip?" she cried.

"Reinaldo just ate it," Trey said.

"Reinaldo? Is that the dog?" Roxy asked.

Trey nodded. Reinaldo looked at Roxy and burped.

"The plot thickens," Roxy said.

"No!" Jane grabbed Reinaldo and started shaking him. "Spit it out! Spit it out!"

"I wouldn't do that if I were you," Trey said. His cell phone rang. "Hello? Hey, *Mom*." He flashed a meaningful look at Roxy.

Uh-oh. The senator. Roxy scanned the room, trying to remember where she'd left her clothes.

"Okay," Trey said. "See you in a minute." He hung up and bolted for the door. He flipped the security lock so no one could get in, key or no key.

"What's wrong?" Roxy asked.

"My mom's on her way up!" Trey said. "Hide!"

7

"Where can we hide?" Roxy asked. "She'll find us! We've got to get out of here!"

Jane dropped the dog onto the bed. "Senator Lipton? She's coming back? Now what do we do?"

Roxy picked up Reinaldo. After all, he had the chip inside him, somewhere. . . .

The dog snarled and squirmed in her arms.

"Let me think, let me think. . . ." Roxy said. "Ow!" She felt a sharp pain in her pinky. Reinaldo had bitten her! She yanked her sore, drool-covered pinky out of Reinaldo's sharp little teeth and tossed the dog to Trey.

"Ow!" he cried. "He bit me too! Stupid dog!"

He tossed the dog back to Roxy. He bit her again! She tossed him to Jane without thinking.

"No!" Jane squealed and ducked. The snarling dog flew through the air and sailed right out the window!

"Ahhhhhh!" Roxy screamed. She'd forgotten—Jane was terrified of dogs. Roxy ran to the window. Jane and Trey were right behind her.

Roxy felt dizzy as she stared down from the ninth-floor window. Where was Reinaldo? How could a dog survive such a long fall? Was he all right?

"Arf!"

"There he is!" Jane cried. She pointed to the window ledge, two rooms away. Reinaldo stood there wagging his tail, unhurt.

Roxy sighed with relief. Now they just had to get him back—somehow.

"Here, boy," Trey called, whistling for the dog. "Here, Reinaldo!"

Reinaldo trotted away along the ledge.

"Hey—get back here, you little rat!" Jane cried. She crawled through the window and onto the ledge, still dressed in her towel.

"Jane, what are you doing?" Roxy asked. "You could fall and kill yourself!"

"Without that chip I'm dead anyway," Jane said.

Clank. Roxy heard a noise at the door. She turned and looked at it. It was open an inch, stopped by the security lock.

"Uh-oh," Trey said. "It's Mom!"

"Trey, why is the door locked?" Senator Lipton called through the tiny opening.

Roxy looked from the door to the window. The idea of meeting the senator after breaking into her room was not appealing. As far as she could see, there was only one way out. "I've got to bolt," she told Trey. "I'm late for a date with Simple Plan."

"The video shoot?" Trey asked.

"Impressive," Roxy said. He knew his music. She climbed out the window and followed Jane along the ledge.

"Here, doggie-dog," Jane coaxed in a baby voice. "What a clever boy. Yes, you are. Come back to Mommy so I can shove my finger down your throat and get that chip."

Reinaldo scampered away and hopped onto a window-washing platform.

They crawled along the ledge after the dog. "Well, he's trapped now. He's got nowhere to go but down."

Jane climbed aboard the platform, clinging to a rope.

Roxy stepped on after her. "You get him," she told Jane. She wasn't eager to pick up Reinaldo after he'd bitten her twice.

Shaking, Jane picked up the dog and held him tightly in her arms. "Got him!" she said. He wagged his tail.

Roxy was amazed—she'd never seen Jane hold a dog before. The lengths Jane would go to for that nerd book of hers . . . "I think he likes you," she said. "And only you."

She glanced up. Trey's handsome head poked out the hotel window.

"We've got him! He's okay!" Roxy called to him. She waved to him and her hand knocked against a red button.

Whoosh! The platform suddenly dropped like an elevator going down. Roxy screamed, her hair flying straight up. The platform jerked to a stop five floors down, and Roxy clung to a rope, catching her breath. "Whew! That was close."

"Roxy—look," Jane pointed to the window in front of them.

Roxy peered through it. In the hotel room, a blondish-gray-haired man in his forties was buttoning a clean pair of pants. Then he picked up a mug of coffee and took a sip.

"Isn't that the guy from the train?" she asked.

"I think so," Jane said.

"I guess he got his pants cleaned," Roxy said. "Good for him."

The man looked up and spotted them through his window. His swollen red eye had turned bruise-purple. "Ahhhh!" he cried, startled. He dropped his mug and spilled coffee all over his pants! "Leave me alone!" he pleaded.

"I guess he recognized us," Roxy said.

The platform suddenly shot down again and screeched to a stop. Roxy looked down. They were at the second floor now. At least it wasn't so far to fall.

"We're at the end of the rope," Jane said. "It won't go down any farther."

Directly below them was a Dumpster filled with garbage bags. Perfect! "We're going to have to jump," Roxy said.

"You're insane!" Jane protested. "I'm not going to—"

Roxy didn't wait to hear the rest. If Jane could handle touching a dog, she could handle this. Roxy jumped off the platform and landed safely on her back onto cushion of garbage.

"Whoa!" Jane cried. Without Roxy balancing her, the platform tipped over. Jane slid off and fell into the garbage with Reinaldo in her arms. "That wasn't so bad," she said.

Roxy stared up at the ninth-floor window they'd started from. "Could have been a lot worse," she agreed.

"Why did you have the door locked?" Senator Lipton demanded once Trey let her into her room.

"Sorry, Mom. I was just taking a nap," he said. He stuck his head out the window again to make sure the girls were all right. Roxy waved to him from a garbage Dumpster. That Roxy sure was cute. And it looked as if nobody was hurt. Not yet anyway. When his mother realized Reinaldo was missing . . . Well, he couldn't even think about it.

"Look what I got my sweet little boy." Senator Lipton held up a big bone-shaped dog biscuit.

"Thanks, Mom, but I already ate," Trey said.

"It's for Reinaldo," the senator said. "Here, Reinaldo! Here, boy! Where are you, my precious angel?" She scanned the room, then checked the bathroom. "Have you seen Reinaldo?" she asked Trey. "He's not answering me! He always answers me."

"Mom, there's something you should know," Trey said.

Senator Lipton's face went gray. "Trey— what is going on here? Where did he go?"

Let's see, Trey thought, his mind racing for a good answer. *Where did he go . . . where did he go. . . .* "I took him, um, to . . . the groomer! Surprise!" *That ought to hold her for a while.*

"Why did you take him to the groomer?" Senator Lipton asked. "He just came back from the groomer yesterday."

Uh-oh, she was suspicious. "He smelled?"

The senator took his face in her hands and broke into a smile. "Trey. I know you, and you're up to something. Maybe that's what smells."

Trey tried to put on his most indignant face. "Wow! That hurts," he said, glancing at her for a reaction. So far, nothing but stone face. He had to keep up the pity tactic. "Can't I do something nice for Reinaldo without getting the third degree?"

He watched her for signs of melting and . . . there. The stone face softened.

"You're right," she said. "I'm sorry." She hugged Trey. "So when can we pick him up?"

"Exactly," Trey said, playing for time. She looked confused, so he parried with, "You know what? I just realized I have a . . . I'm late for the . . . you know the thing, with that group at the place."

Trey was out of lies—he couldn't hang on much longer. He threw open the door and bolted out of the room. *Better get out of here before she catches on.*

He raced down the hall to the elevator and jabbed the Down button. He had to catch those girls and get Reinaldo back—or his mom would go Terminator on him. "Come on come on come on," he muttered impatiently. Finally, sick of waiting for the elevator, he dashed down the stairs. If he didn't get that dog back, he was a dead man.

"Hold Reinaldo." Jane handed the dog to Roxy, who had jumped out of the Dumpster and stood waiting for her on the ground. She climbed out of the trash and straightened her towel. She dusted herself off as best she could. She'd just taken a shower—and now she was all garbage-y! She glanced at Roxy in her short white robe. It didn't seem to bother *her*.

Roxy set Reinaldo on the ground.

"What are you doing?" Jane asked. "We need that dog!"

"We need to leave," Roxy said.

"Right now that dog is my life," Jane said. "And when he poops, his poop is my life!" She took a deep breath, trying to compose herself. She couldn't believe it had all come to *this*—waiting for a dog to go to the bathroom. Her day planner was being held hostage by a thug who wanted a microchip, which had been eaten by a dog. Getting her day planner—and the McGill Fellowship speech—back depended completely on this ugly, overgroomed dog!

She picked up Reinaldo. She wasn't overly fond of dogs, but she could put her dislike aside temporarily for the sake of her day planner. "Let's go," she said. "We've got to meet Bennie in fifteen minutes." She marched out of the hotel alley and into the busy street.

"Jane, watch out!" Roxy shouted.

Jane turned toward the traffic. A bike was speeding toward her, about to hit her!

"Ahhhhh!" Jane dropped Reinaldo and braced herself for the impact. The biker braked hard and flew over the handlebars. He landed right on top of her!

Oof! A heavy weight pressed Jane to the ground. She opened her eyes and looked up. A face stared down at her. She blinked. It was the cute guy from the train station. The one whose bike chain had torn her skirt! She'd thought he was gone forever, but here he was again, like magic. *Wow!* she thought. *He looks even cuter up close!*

"Am I squashing you?" he asked.

"I don't mind," Jane said. She froze. "Um, did I just—"

"Yeah. You said that out loud." He grinned and helped her to her feet.

Jane blushed and adjusted her towel. What a way to run into him! She wished she'd been better dressed—or even somewhat dressed. "You know, one of us could get hurt if we keep doing this."

"I know," he said. "But I like running into you."

"I like running into you too," Jane said. The rest of the world seemed to fall away. For a moment she forgot all about Reinaldo and Roxy and Bennie and the fellowship. . . .

"I'm Jim."

"I'm Jane."

"Oh, *God!*" Roxy interjected. She'd picked up the dog. "Her number is 516-555-8989. She's home. Every night. Call her." She grabbed Jane's hand. "Jane, we've got to get going."

That's right—her day planner. She stole a last glance at Jim and hurried down the street after Roxy. *I hope he calls*, she thought.

Lomax muttered to himself. He sat in his car at 59th Street and Ninth Avenue, across the street from a roped-off alley where a film crew was getting ready for a video shoot. He had a CB radio, a police scanner, and a box of doughnuts on the dashboard. He was ready for anything. He had driven through rush hour traffic all the way in from Long Island and waited all morning for Roxy Ryan to show up. But so far, nothing. Where was she?

He watched the activity through his binoculars. He eyed the trailers for the band and the director, camera trucks, and film crew milling around. Lots of kids dressed in those ripped-up clothes they liked so much— leather, jeans, weird hair colors, pierced noses . . . *Disgusting*, Lomax thought.

Two beefy guards stood at a security station just outside the alley. They checked names off on a clipboard and moved a rope aside to let people onto the set.

Maybe she's already inside, Lomax thought. *In any case, I'd be surprised if that alley wasn't crawling with truants like ants on a Popsicle stick.* He set down his binoculars and got out of his car. "Let's go crack some skulls," he said to himself and sauntered across the street. He headed for the alley, but a security guard stopped him at the entrance.

"Where do you think you're going?" the guard asked.

Lomax flashed his truant officer badge. "I'm on a case, Einstein. Where do you think *you're* going?"

"What do you mean?" the guard asked. "I'm not going anywhere."

"So we're clear on that," Lomax said.

"Huh?" the guard grunted.

"I didn't think so," Lomax said. He stepped around the guard, who was too confused to stop him. Worked every time.

If she's not here yet, she will be soon, Lomax thought, looking around. *All I have to do is wait.*

• • •

I wish I had some clothes, Jane thought as she raced down the street with Roxy. People were staring at them. And it was hard to keep the towel on while holding a dog and running as fast as you could.

They jogged through the crowds, which got thicker the closer they got to Central Park and the Plaza Hotel. They passed a street vendor with a cart selling I ♥ NY souvenirs. Jane screeched to a halt.

"Why are we stopping?" Roxy asked.

"Look," Jane said. The cart displayed hats, tank tops, halters, shorts, underwear, and sneakers. Perfect. "Sir," Jane said to the vendor, "want to make a deal?"

The vendor stared at her and smiled. "You need clothes!" he said. "I sell clothes!"

The problem was, they didn't have any money. They didn't have anything but the dog, and they needed him. Then Jane's alarm watch beeped. Aha!

"I'll trade you this watch for two sets of clothes," Jane offered. "T-shirts, shorts, and sneakers. Deal?"

"I don't want to wear that stuff!" Roxy complained. "That's for tourists!"

Roxy and I had
an important day
ahead of us in
New York City.
We each had our
own plans...

We had no idea we'd end up spending the day together.

Our adventure began with a chase through the subway.
Roxy helped us escape with some impressive kung fu moves.

The day only seemed to get worse when we were soaked by a passing car.

The video shoot Roxy went to was amazing until Officer Lomax busted her!

After escaping Officer Lomax, Roxy and I needed a
fashion change.

Can you imagine us running around New York City like this?

Now we had one more thing to figure out—which way to Columbia University?

I made it just on time to give my speech.

But so did Lomax.

Think it all worked out for me and Roxy?
Hey, anything can happen in a New York minute!

"Would you rather run around town in a bathrobe all day?" Jane asked.

"Never mind," Roxy said.

The vendor looked at the watch. "Okay. Deal."

The girls slipped behind the cart to put on their new clothes. Jane set Reinaldo down. He started sniffing the sidewalk.

"Hey, maybe he's about to go!" Roxy said.

They got dressed while Reinaldo sniffed around.

"Thanks," Jane said to the vendor. "Any luck yet?" she asked Roxy, who was watching Reinaldo.

"We're working on it," Roxy reported as the dog circled and stopped, sniffing one spot in particular. "Hold on. We may have something."

Come on, Reinaldo, Jane thought. *We need that chip!* Her heart started beating fast. It did that sometimes when she got anxious—and right now she was about as anxious as she'd ever been in her life. Reinaldo walked on.

"False alarm," Roxy said.

Jane clutched her chest. She couldn't take the tension any longer. "Oh, God, my heart's starting to palpitate!"

"Jane, relax," Roxy said. "Everything's going to work out fine."

That's what Roxy always said. She must have said it five times already that day, and she hadn't been right yet—not once.

"Yeah, crazy ol' me," Jane snapped. "Overreacting again. I'm glad I actually have clothes to wear now. But do you think I can show up for my presentation looking like this?" She glanced down at her white tank top and shorts, covered with red I ♥ NY logos. She looked ridiculous.

Roxy shrugged. "I guess they'll just think you really love New York."

"Very funny." Jane would try to find some better clothes later—once she got her day planner back. She picked up Reinaldo and started walking.

"Where are you going?" Roxy asked.

"To get my day planner," Jane said.

"I'm not letting you go alone," Roxy said. "Not after what we've been through."

"Look, Bennie just wants his stupid chip back," Jane said, "and after the luck we've had working as a team, I'd rather go this one alone. Have fun at the rock concert." She stormed off toward the Plaza Hotel. Maybe without Roxy around she could straighten things out and actually make it to Columbia for her presentation.

"It's a video shoot!" Roxy called after her.

Whatever, Jane thought.

She found the Plaza Hotel on 59th Street and Fifth Avenue. It was big and beautiful and right across the street from Central Park. Well-dressed people flowed through the revolving doors. A stream of black limos lined the entrance. Jane walked past them, peering into the drivers' windows, looking for Bennie. How would she ever find him among so many limos?

She reached the corner and heard a honk coming from a parked limo. Bennie stepped out, scowling. "You're late."

Now that she was face-to-face with the huge man, her bravado faded, and she began to babble nervously. "Look," she began, "I think we all got off on the wrong foot awhile back, so I'm willing to start over if you are. I just want to say that I really appreciate your returning my day planner so promptly and—Whoa!"

Bennie yanked her by one arm and shoved her into the back of the limo. He climbed in beside her and closed the door. "Give me the chip," he demanded.

"Here." Jane handed him Reinaldo.

"What's this?" Bennie asked.

"It's your chip," Jane replied.

"Excuse me?"

"Reinaldo ate your chip," Jane explained.

"Reinaldo ate my chip. Is that a joke?"

"I don't joke," Jane said.

Bennie took the dog and stared at its face. Then he shook it, first left to right, then up and down. Nothing happened. "Maybe I should run the dog over," he said.

"No!" Jane cried. So what if she didn't like dogs. She didn't want Reinaldo to be crushed! She glanced around the back seat of the limo, searching for something she could use as a weapon or a distraction.

"You're right," Bennie said. "That might damage the chip." He put his huge face right up to Reinaldo's tiny one. "Give me my chip or I'll kill you!"

Jane heard a hissing sound and looked down. Reinaldo was peeing on Bennie's jacket! *Good dog*, she thought.

"Ugh! Stop that!" Bennie yelled, dropping the dog.

Now was her chance. As Bennie frantically tried to wipe the dog pee off his jacket, Jane scooped up Reinaldo and hurried out of the car. "Nice shooting, Reinaldo," she said.

Reinaldo barked as if he understood.

Jane ran down the street. She glanced back and saw Bennie stumble out of the limo, shaking his jacket. "I think we can slip away, Reinaldo." She turned a corner and dashed down 59th Street. "I'll just have to live without my day planner for now." She needed it, but maybe it wasn't worth dying for after all. "Let's go find Roxy."

8

"Cool," Roxy said as she surveyed the set of the video shoot. The alley off 59th Street had been transformed with lights, a stage, a raised mosh pit, a dance floor just below it, and hundreds of extras.

Roxy flashed her All Access badge at the security guard, who let her in. Just in time too. The video director—a short, plump, coffee-skinned guy with dreadlocks—bounded onstage.

"Are you ready to rock?" he prompted. The crowd cheered and whistled. "We're running multiple cameras today, so just act naturally. Give it up for Simple Plan!"

The crowd went crazy as Simple Plan took the stage. The lead singer, Jack, grabbed the microphone and started singing Roxy's favorite song, "Vacation."

All right, Roxy thought, grooving to the music. *Time to put my All Access pass to work.* She ran up a ramp that led backstage. A guard stopped her, but she flashed her badge again and he let her go. *Thank you, Justin*, she thought. Then she spotted some middle-aged guys in expensive suits dancing like dorks—totally rhythmically challenged. *Old-school dance moves. Must be the A-and-R guys.*

Too bad Roxy didn't have any CDs to give them—she'd left her bag back in Trey's hotel room. But she could still talk them up a bit, wow them with her charm, and get their office addresses so she could drop off a CD later. She beelined toward a cluster of suits when someone called, "Roxy!"

She stopped, and Trey ran up to her. "Hey! What's up, Trey?"

"I was trying to find you," Trey said. "I see you found some clothes."

Roxy glanced down at her cheesy tourist wear. Why did he have to see her in this?

"It's not my style, but it looks cute on you," Trey said. He handed her her bag. "You left this in the hotel."

"Excellent!" Roxy said. "Thanks, Trey." *That was nice of him. He went to all this trouble just to return my bag? Or is there more to it than that?* She hoped there was.

"There's something else," Trey said, and Roxy smiled. *Yes!* "I thought you might know where my mom's dog is."

Roxy's good mood deflated. So that was what he wanted.

"I also wanted to see you again," he added.

Yes! That was more like it. "My sister has him," she said. "I think I know where to find her. Just let me pass out a few of my CDs to some of these A-and-R guys and we'll go."

"You have a CD?" Trey asked.

"Just a demo," Roxy replied. "I play drums in a band."

"Excellent," Trey said. He took a CD and looked at it. "Hot cover," he said, glancing from the glammed-up photo of Roxy to the real thing.

Roxy blushed and wished again that she was wearing cooler clothes. Oh, well. What could she do about it now? She and Trey made their way to the dorky guys in suits.

Roxy introduced herself to the record company guys and handed out some CDs. Then she spotted someone talking to a groupie in the corner. His back was to her, but it was a familiar back. An older man in a uniform that almost looked like a cop's but wasn't quite.

Oh, no. Was it Lomax? How had he traced her here?

"Wait here a second," she said to Trey. "I'll be right back." She moved closer to the man to make sure she was right. "How come you're not in school today?" the man was asking the groupie.

"Get lost," the groupie snapped.

Then the man turned around. It *was* Lomax! And he'd spotted her!

"The jig is up, Ryan," Lomax said. "There's nowhere to go."

Roxy couldn't help but look around for an escape route anyway.

Lomax hooked his thumbs into his belt and leaned back on his heels. "I have to say, Roxanne, it's been quite a chase all these years. There've been a few clever moves on your part. . . ."

Roxy kept herself from rolling her eyes. She had no idea Lomax had been so obsessed with her all this time. While he talked, the wheels in her mind were turning. There had to be a way out of this—all she had to do was find it. She scanned Lomax from head to toe. There had to be a weak spot somewhere.

"But slow and steady wins the race," Lomax went on. "And, alas, here we are."

What a weirdo, Roxy thought. "You're right," she told him. "I'm tired of running. This had to end sometime."

Lomax's eyebrows shot up in surprise, and Roxy suppressed a grin. "I'll go quietly," she said. She held out her hands as if waiting for Lomax to handcuff her. "But first, you may want to zip up your fly."

Lomax's eyes dropped to his pants zipper. Roxy dashed away, slipped between a pair of giant speakers, and disappeared into the group watching the band from backstage. She glanced behind her. A security guard was blocking Lomax's way to the stage. That would buy her a few minutes.

But where could she go? She had only two choices—back toward Lomax or onto the stage. Roxy wasn't shy. She'd take the stage over Lomax any day.

She walked onto the stage and stood behind the bassist. The people dancing and moshing in the audience started waving and cheering her. Jack looked back and grinned at her, nodding his approval.

She glanced at Lomax. He was arguing with the security guard, but if she knew Lomax, he'd find a way to get past the guard soon. Desperate to create a diversion, she started jumping up and down to the music.

The crowd followed her lead and started jumping up and down too. Soon the whole place was pogo-ing like crazy. The moshers moshed harder, and a few guys rushed the stage and climbed up. The band rocked out, and the stage was mobbed with fans jumping up and down. Roxy hoped Lomax would lose her in the crowd.

"Roxy!" She heard someone calling her name. Jane! The crowd had pressed Jane against the front of the stage. She jumped up and down, clutching Reinaldo and yelling, "Help!"

"Jane!" Roxy shouted. She reached down and took Reinaldo with one hand. With the other she helped Jane up to the stage.

"Come on, dance!" Roxy said. "Blend in!" She moved her hips to show Jane what she meant, since her sister was more than a little stiff on the dance floor. "What are you doing here?" she shouted to Jane over the music.

"Looking for you," Jane said.

Roxy was surprised—and touched. "Really? I thought I was bad luck."

"Roxy!" another voice shouted. It was Trey, pushing his way across the dance floor. He waved and pointed at Reinaldo. Roxy nodded and waited for him to reach the stage. The band went right into another hard-rocking song, and Roxy bobbed her head to the beat. Jane danced beside her, slowly loosening up. She was even smiling. *She's actually enjoying herself!* Roxy realized.

Roxy turned to the rowdy crowd. A flash of silver caught her eye. A badge! It was Lomax! Roxy stopped dancing for a second. Lomax was holding out his badge and pushing through the crowd toward the stage.

"What's wrong?" Jane asked.

"Lomax," Roxy said.

"Lomax?" Jane asked.

Of course, Roxy thought. *Miss Goody-Goody Jane wouldn't know who Lomax was. She'd never missed a day of school in her life.*

"The truant officer," Roxy explained. "He's coming this way!"

Lomax had obviously spotted her. He had

finally made it to the stage and was trying to climb up the side.

Okay, so we'll run backstage and slip away from him, Roxy thought. But when she glanced backstage, there stood Bennie like a brick wall blocking their way out. He waved at her and Jane.

"Bennie!" Jane gasped. "How do we get out of this? We're trapped!"

Roxy surveyed the situation and saw the quickest way out—crowd-surfing. "Hold my hand!" she told Jane. She took Jane's hand and dove into the crowd of dancers. Reinaldo slipped out of Roxy's arms.

"Ahhhhh!" Jane screamed as the crowd passed Roxy and Jane over their heads from person to person toward the back of the dance floor.

This is excellent! Roxy thought. Before she knew it, she was passed right into Trey's hands.

"Where's Reinaldo?" Trey asked.

"I don't know!" Roxy replied as the crowd surfed her along to the next person. She looked back and spotted Reinaldo. He was crowd-surfing too! "There he is!" Roxy shouted to Trey, but he couldn't hear her. So

Roxy called to Jane, who was right next to her, "Grab Reinaldo!"

Jane swiped the dog out of the sweaty crowd and held him as she surfed. She caught a whiff of body odor and wrinkled her nose. "Ever hear of deodorant?" she asked one of the dancers.

They reached the back of the dance floor, landing gently on their feet. Roxy searched the crowd for Lomax. He was standing on the stage.

He spotted her and dove onto the dance floor to crowd-surf. "Geronimo!" he shouted.

But nobody caught him, and he landed on the floor with a thud. Face-plant. Bennie teetered on the edge of the stage, gloomily staring at Lomax on the floor.

"Let's get out of here," Roxy said. Trey would just have to wait a little longer to get Reinaldo back. They dashed out of the alley and ran down the street without stopping for three blocks. Finally, out of breath, Roxy stopped to look back.

"I think we lost them," Jane said.

"Good," Roxy said. "We've got to get back to the video shoot."

"What?" Jane asked. "No way."

"Trey's looking for the dog," Roxy explained.

"We can't," Jane protested. "Bennie is after me and the dog again. Didn't you see him backstage?"

"Roxanne Ryan, it's over. There's nowhere to run!" a voice boomed. Roxy looked around. Lomax! He was only a block away!

"He's like the Terminator!" Roxy said. "Run!"

Trey raced to the alley entrance, trying to catch up with Roxy and Jane. Why were they always running away from him? He had to get Reinaldo back or his mother would go ballistic!

He looked up and down the street. No sign of them.

"Dude, I'm looking for two blond girls and a little dog that just ran out of here," Trey said to the security guard. "Did you see where they went?"

The guard shrugged, but a beefy man in a chauffeur's outfit said, "I did. They went to the after party."

After party! "Great," he muttered. How could Roxy do that to him when she knew how much he needed to get Reinaldo back?

"I'm heading over there," the chauffeur said. "I drive all the VIPs. Come on."

"Thanks," Trey said. He followed the man to a long black limo.

The chauffeur opened the trunk. "I just have to get a package from the trunk," the chauffeur said.

So? Trey thought, waiting for him to open the back door of the limo.

"It's a very big package," the chauffeur explained. "Very heavy too. Could you give me a hand?"

Whatever, Trey thought, but he said, "Uh, sure." He walked to the trunk and looked inside. "Whoa!" The chauffeur picked him up and dumped him into the trunk. "Dude, what are you—"

The trunk lid slammed shut. Trey lay on the floor in total darkness.

"Hey!" Trey shouted, banging on the trunk lid as hard as he could. "Hey! Let me out of here! Help! HELP!"

9

"Who knew an old guy like that could run so fast?" Jane said. Lomax was hard on their heels, and there was no place to hide.

"What about that tent?" Roxy said.

A blue tent loomed ahead, the kind city workers used to keep people away when they were digging up the street or working on underground pipes.

Jane didn't think it was a great idea, but there was nowhere else to go. She heard Lomax's voice outside the tent. "Halt in the name of the law!" he shouted.

"Let's go!" Jane cried and they quickly dived into the tent. Whoa! The ground suddenly dropped out from under their feet!

Splash! Jane landed in a deep pool of water. Her eyes adjusted to the darkness. Sunlight beamed down from a hole above them.

They'd fallen through a hole in the street and landed in some kind of water pipe!

Jane checked Reinaldo to see if he was all right. He was. "Roxy, are you okay?" she asked.

"Fine," Roxy said. "But we can't stop now. Lomax might have seen us. Start moving!"

Jane and Roxy waded through the waist-deep water. Jane looked around for signs of sludge. Her breathing grew faster. She was starting to hyperventilate again. With all this craziness going on, she'd almost forgotten about the McGill Fellowship!

"The climactic event of my academic career is in two hours!" she cried. "And I'm wading in a sewer!"

"It's just a water main, Jane." Roxy pointed out a sign stamped on the pipe wall: NYC DEPARTMENT OF WATER. "We're in luck."

Luck? What planet was Roxy living on? They were running from a psychopath and a crazed truant officer and were trapped in a tunnel of water, soaking wet, dirty, and wearing I ♥ NY souvenirs! She gave her sister a look.

"What?" Roxy said. "I'm just trying to look on the bright side."

"Bright side?" Jane screeched. "Let me

tell you something, Rox. Short of someone handing me a snorkel right now, there is no bright side! In fact, nothing about this entire day has had even the remotest hint of a bright side! Zip. *Nada. Niente!*"

"I don't know," Roxy said. "I was sort of thinking that . . ."

"That what?" Jane asked, still impatient.

"Well, that it's been years since we've actually spent a whole day together. You know, just you and me." She paused and smiled a little. "And don't tell me you didn't have any fun at the video shoot. I saw that look on your face when we were dancing."

"I was acting for the cameras," Jane insisted, though deep down she knew it was a big, fat lie.

Apparently so did Roxy, who raised a skeptical eyebrow.

"All right, maybe it was a little fun," Jane admitted. At least it was a nice change of pace from running for her life. "Except for that Lomax guy giving me the creeps. What's with him, anyway?"

Roxy rolled her eyes. "I figured you wouldn't know who he was. He's a truant officer. Been after me for years."

"Years?" Jane knew Roxy had cut a lot of school, but she had no idea it was this bad.

Roxy shrugged. "I always outsmart him. What can I say?"

Jane shook her head. "You're insane, you know that?"

"Yeah, I am," Roxy agreed. She nudged Jane with an elbow until Jane finally smiled.

It wasn't so bad spending a day with Roxy—even a total disaster like this day.

They trudged for blocks through the water. At least there was no sign of Lomax or Bennie. *Maybe we've lost them at last*, Jane thought.

"I need to get out of here," Jane said. "This pipe is never ending."

"Wait a second," Roxy said. "You said Columbia is on 116th Street, right?"

Jane nodded. Roxy pointed to some numbers painted on an overhead pipe: 125TH STREET.

"I got you nine blocks away," Roxy said.

Well, it was something. "There's a ladder," Jane said. She crawled up the ladder until her head bumped against something metal—a manhole cover. "Help me push this thing open," Jane said.

Together they pushed against the manhole until it popped up. It clanked onto the pavement. Jane poked her head up. They were near the curb of a street. Cars whizzed past their heads.

Jane crawled out of the water main, followed by Roxy. She looked around for a street sign.

"We're on 125th Street and Lexington Avenue," Roxy said.

Jane's heart sank. Lexington Avenue was in East Harlem—nowhere near Columbia University. "Roxy, Columbia's on the west side of town," Jane said.

"So I made a mistake." Roxy shrugged. "Did you want to slosh around in that water any longer?"

"No," Jane said. "Maybe we can catch a taxi." She spotted one parked across the street. Then she noticed the building behind it. It was painted bright pink and gold, with a big window looking out onto the street. A pink sign said BIG SHIRL'S HOUSE OF BLING in gold letters.

"Wow," Roxy gasped. "Check it out."

"It's a beauty salon," Jane said. "Maybe they can help me get cleaned up for my presentation!"

Inside was just as amazing as the outside. There were racks of sparkly, colorful clothes. Six women sat in barber chairs having their hair made into fabulous, towering hairdos. A young man sat near the door, reading a magazine. Jane figured he might be the driver of the cab parked outside. Hip-hop music played on the radio. Jane had never seen a beauty salon like it, but she had to admit it was beautiful.

Jane and Roxy opened the door. A little bell jangled above them. Everybody turned to stare at them. The women were covered with big gold jewelry, wore lots of makeup, and had long, elaborate fingernails.

Jane suddenly felt uncomfortable. What was she thinking? This was no place to clean up for an academic presentation. Everybody here was so glitzy. And why should she expect a group of total strangers to help her anyway?

"We're *so* not in Kansas anymore," Jane whispered to Reinaldo.

In their soaking wet I ♥ NY T-shirts and red shorts, Jane and Roxy didn't exactly fit in. They'd been through the wringer and it showed. Glitzy they weren't.

A large, intimidating woman, the biggest

one in the room, put down the sandwich she was eating. "May I help you?" she asked the girls.

She must be Big Shirl, Jane thought. This woman was clearly the boss.

Roxy turned to Jane and said, "Hey, this isn't Radio City Music Hall! Sorry, she has a terrible sense of direction," she said to Big Shirl. "See ya!"

Jane was surprised. It wasn't like Roxy to be so nervous. The girls turned to go.

"Hold it!" Big Shirl called out.

Jane and Roxy turned back to face her.

"I can't have anyone seeing you leave my shop looking like that," Big Shirl said. "Go out the back way."

"Yes ma'am," Jane and Roxy said at once. Something about Big Shirl made you obey her. The girls walked through the salon toward the back.

Jane glanced up and saw a clock. Her heart nearly stopped. It was 1:13! "Ahhhh!" she screamed. She had less than two hours until her presentation!

"What? What is it?" Roxy asked.

"It's 1:13!" Jane shrieked. She started hyperventilating again. "It's 1:13, it's 1:13, it's 1:13!

I'm never going to make it. I'm never going to make it. . . ."

"What's wrong with that girl?" Big Shirl asked.

"She has a problem with pressure," Roxy explained.

Jane clutched her chest. It felt tight and she was having trouble breathing. She doubled over. "Oh my God. Oh my God. I'm having a heart attack!" she gasped. "I'm having a heart attack! Call 911!"

She felt dizzy. The room started to swirl. A woman screamed. Then—*splash!*—somebody threw water into her face.

"I said I needed an ambulance, not a shower!" Jane sputtered. "Oh, God, my arm's going numb!"

"I swear, she was just fine a minute ago," Roxy said. She stared into Jane's eyes. "Jane, it's me, Roxy."

"Who's Jane?" Jane said. The room was still spinning. She didn't know where she was. Her mind felt numb. "I don't know Jane. Why are you calling me Jane?"

Roxy stroked her hair. "Come on, stay with me now, Jane. Take deep breaths and think happy thoughts. You can do it."

Jane's breathing slowed a little. The room stopped spinning, but she still felt panicky.

"Here, sing with me." Roxy started singing, "The itsy-bitsy spider went up the water spout. . . ."

Jane mustered the strength to sing along. "Down came the rain and washed the spider out." Slowly she began to catch her breath, and her mind cleared. She looked around. Oh, yeah. She was in that beauty parlor. Big Shirl's.

"Out came the sun and dried up all the rain," she sang with Roxy. "So the itsy-bitsy spider went up the spout again."

Ah. Okay. Much better now.

"Works every time," Roxy said to Big Shirl. "She'll be fine now."

"Damn," Big Shirl said. "I was so hoping for an encore of 'Row, Row, Row Your Boat.'"

Jane pouted. There was no need for sarcasm, as far as she was concerned. She couldn't help it if she got panicky sometimes.

"You mind telling me what that was all about?" Big Shirl demanded.

Jane took a deep breath. "In less than two hours I'm supposed to give the most important speech of my life."

119

"Well, I sure hope you can talk better than you can sing," Big Shirl snapped. The other women in the salon giggled.

Jane whimpered and started to double over again. Why did Big Shirl have to pick on her?

Roxy came to her rescue. "I'm not entirely sure that was helpful. Jane's had sort of a rough day."

"So who hasn't?" Big Shirl said. "That's a part of life, sweetheart. Heck, if it was all smooth sailing, you know where we'd be? Bored to tears, that's where. Sit down." She grabbed Jane by the shoulders and manhandled her into an empty barber chair.

Jane stared into the mirror while Big Shirl started fiddling with her wet, lank blond hair. Jane felt so helpless and hopeless she didn't have the energy to resist.

"It's the curve balls that make life interesting," Big Shirl said. "Shows us what we're made of. And sometimes, if we're real lucky, there's a blessing waiting for us at the end of that wrong turn."

Jane looked at her reflection. God, she looked a mess. Every disaster she'd been through that day seemed to show somewhere on her body. "What if it's been about fifty wrong turns?" she asked.

"Well, your last one brought you in here, now didn't it?" Big Shirl replied. "So, honey, prepare to be blessed. Mickey," she called to the young man sitting by the door. "Bring me my toolbox, baby. We've got some major bling to do."

She smiled at Jane. Roxy's face appeared in the mirror beside her. She smiled and waved at Jane. Jane waved back and began to relax. She was in good hands with Big Shirl. But she did have one question. "Who's Major Bling?" Jane asked.

"Honey, this is Big Shirl's House of Bling. This is where the bling is born. This is where bling lives."

Works for me, Jane thought with a shrug.

Big Shirl flashed a huge smile. "You've got nothing to worry about." She pointed to a barber chair next to Jane's, and Roxy sat down. "Girls, let's get to work," she said to her team of stylists.

"I'll do the ugly little dog," one of the stylists offered. "He needs some serious bling. Or something."

Big Shirl started braiding Jane's hair. Jane

hoped Shirl wouldn't make her look too funky. She had a feeling the McGill Fellowship committee wasn't big on bling. "Uh, just so we're clear, I need a more corporate bling," Jane said.

"No problem, honey," Big Shirl said. "Big Shirl can do it all."

Jane sat still while stylists washed her hair, styled it, dried it, and started over again. First they braided her hair into elaborate corn rows.

"Not quite working," Jane said.

"You're right, honey," Big Shirl agreed.

Jane glanced at Roxy, whose blond hair was worked into big, ribbon-y loops. Reinaldo had a tiny blue Mohawk on top of his head.

"Try again, girls!" Big Shirl ordered, and they went through the whole process once more.

At last Jane's hair was blown dry into pretty, conservative curls. "Perfect!" she declared.

Roxy's hair was punked out and spiky, and Reinaldo had a blue ribbon tied around his neck.

"I can't do much with him," Reinaldo's

stylist admitted. "He's just one butt-ugly dog."

"And now for some threads." Big Shirl flipped through a rack of clothes and brought out a short mod dress for Jane and red sequins for Roxy. Jane tried on her dress and modeled it for everyone.

"You look *hot*," Roxy said.

"Excellent!" Jane cried, studying herself in the mirror. It wasn't her usual conservative self, but it had a lot of personality. Maybe *too much* personality, but she could work with it.

Big Shirl held out her right hand, and Jane slapped it five. "All right!" Big Shirl howled, shimmying with happiness. "You sisters look fine! Big Shirl has saved the day!"

"Thanks, Big Shirl," Jane said, "for everything. I promise I'll send you some money to pay for all this the minute I get my day planner back."

Big Shirl grinned. "Honey, it's on the house." Jane and Roxy hugged her. "Mickey, take them wherever they need to go," Big Shirl added to the young man, who was apparently her son.

Mickey stood by the door talking on the shop's pay phone, in the middle of what looked like a very private conversation.

"Mickey!" Big Shirl called again.

"One sec, Mama, I'm on the phone," Mickey called back. He twirled his key chain around his finger.

Then Roxy's cell phone rang. "Hello?" Roxy said. She listened for a second and said to Jane, "It's for you."

Jane took the phone. "This is Jane Ryan speaking."

Bennie's deep voice said, "I've got your boyfriend."

A chill ran through Jane at the sound of Bennie's voice. *Stay calm*, she told herself. "I don't have a boyfriend," Jane said.

"You don't?" Bennie sounded confused for a second. "Well, then I have your sister's boyfriend."

What was he talking about? "She doesn't have one, either," Jane said.

Bennie sighed. "Now you listen and listen good. Meet me at Times Square—47th and Broadway—in twenty minutes. Or else I burn the book." He hung up.

Jane's good mood vanished. She started shaking.

"What did he say?" Roxy asked.

"He's going to burn my book!" Jane cried.

"He can't do that," Roxy said. "That's censorship."

Jane took Reinaldo in her arms. "We've got to go," she said to Big Shirl. "Thanks again for everything."

"Bye, girls." Big Shirl waved as they walked out of the shop. "Good luck!"

They stepped out onto the sidewalk. "How are we going to get downtown?" Jane asked. She looked down the street. About three blocks away she spotted a familiar silhouette—a skinny man in a blue not-quite-police uniform.

"Oh, no," she said to Roxy. "It's Lomax!"

10

Roxy turned to Big Shirl, who stood in the doorway of her shop. "Big Shirl, we need to get out of Dodge—fast!"

Big Shirl peered down the street. Lomax had spotted them and was headed their way. "Stop right there!" he shouted. "Both of you!"

"Looks like you girls are in trouble," Big Shirl said. She turned toward Mickey, who was still on the phone. She snatched his car keys from his hand and tossed them to Jane.

"Cab's around the corner!" Big Shirl cried. "Go!"

Roxy dashed around the corner, Jane right behind her. The cab sat waiting for them. Roxy opened the passenger door and jumped in. Jane stood at the driver's door, staring at the keys in her hand. What was Jane's problem?

"What are you waiting for?" Roxy cried. "Get in!"

Jane got in and put the keys into the ignition. Then she hesitated again.

"Start the car, Jane," Roxy said.

Jane started the car and pressed the gas. The car lurched forward, then slammed to a stop. "I can't do this," she said.

"It's not the time, Jane!" Roxy cried. She stared through the windshield. Lomax was racing up the block. He was almost there!

"I'm not really a very strong driver—" Jane began.

All right, that was it. No more fooling around. Roxy buckled up.

Lomax hurtled his skinny body toward the car and pounded on the window. "Out of the car, Ryan!" he shouted. "I have you surrounded!"

"BRAKE LEFT, GAS RIGHT, GO!" Roxy shouted. She stepped on Jane's right foot, slamming down the gas pedal. The car peeled out, tires squealing.

Jane gripped the steering wheel so hard, her knuckles turned white. "What do I do?!"

"Swerve!" Roxy told her. She grabbed the wheel and yanked it as hard as she could to the left. They just missed mowing down Lomax.

"That was close," Roxy said. "Too close."

Lomax watched the taxi speed downtown. "Dang it all," he muttered. How did that girl always manage to slip away?

He wasn't about to give up. Across the street he noticed a big Winnebago recreational vehicle idling by a fire hydrant. You didn't see many of those in New York City.

A man and a woman stood outside the camper, studying a big map of New York. They had to be out-of-towners. And out-of-towners meant easy marks. Lomax moved closer.

"This can't be Times Square, honey," the man said. "There aren't enough lights."

"Did we take a wrong turn?" his wife asked.

Lomax ran over to the couple, flashing his badge. "Nassau County Department of Truancy. I'm going to have to take over your vehicle. Official business."

Using his most intimidating swagger, Lomax walked right into the Winnebago and sat in the driver's seat. He glanced back at the tourist couple, who shrugged and followed him aboard.

The man sat in the front passenger seat

while his wife hovered behind him. "Tim Brooger," he said, offering Lomax his hand. "My wife, Steffi."

Lomax nodded grimly at them. Lomax didn't have time for pleasantries—he had to catch those girls. He planted his foot on the gas and the Winnebago took off.

"We've never been in a car chase before," Steffi said brightly.

"I think New York has the best car chases," Tim added. "Don't you, honey?"

"Tim?" Lomax snapped. "Put a sock in it."

"Done, sir." Tim made a zipping motion across his lips.

The Winnebago lurched through the city streets. Lomax spotted a yellow taxi up ahead. Was that the one?

"I don't know if this would be helpful," Steffi put in, "but we do have a loudspeaker."

"We use it for campfire sing-a-longs," Tim said. He held out a microphone wired to the dashboard. "Oops—I wasn't supposed to talk, was I?"

"Give me that." Lomax grabbed the mic from Tim. He pulled closer to the yellow taxi. Aha—in the front seat bobbed two blond heads. Ryan! He had her now.

• • •

"Jane, red light!" Roxy cried. Jane slammed on the brake, and the taxi jerked to a stop. "What are you trying to do, make me sick?" she demanded. "How you got your driver's license is beyond me."

Jane said nothing. Roxy thought she saw a guilty frown on her sister's face.

"Oh. My. God," Roxy said. "You failed your driver's test. Unbelievable!"

"I aced the written section!" Jane cried. "I just didn't pass the driving part."

Roxy couldn't believe it. Jane, Miss Perfect who never got anything but straight As her whole life, had failed her driving test!

"Roxanne Ryan! It's all over!" a voice boomed over a loudspeaker.

Roxy checked the rearview mirror. A huge Winnebago was closing in on them.

"Give it up," the voice came from the Winnebago. "Pull over!"

She'd know that voice anywhere. Lomax! She turned around. Sure enough, Lomax was behind the wheel of the Winnebago, right on their tail. And he was sitting with two geeky-looking people she'd never seen before.

"What's going on?" Jane asked.

"Lomax is after us in a giant geek-mobile," Roxy said. "Quick turn left onto Lexington!"

Jane turned onto Lexington and slammed to a stop at a red light. Roxy impatiently glared at the light. *Come on, turn green!*

The door to the back seat opened, and a man jumped into the cab. He wore a suit, carried a briefcase and a cup of coffee, and had a black eye. Roxy did a double take. It was the executive guy from the train and the hotel who kept spilling coffee on himself!

"Okay, I need to get to—" He looked up and saw Jane and Roxy in the front seat. "Oh, my God."

Roxy gave him a little wave. Then the light turned green. "FLOOR IT!" she shouted. Jane pounded the gas, and the car took off.

"You're only making this worse, Ryan!" Lomax blared over the loudspeaker. "You'll be in detention for the rest of your teenage life," he said into the mic. "Let's end this thing right here, right now."

Tim tapped on Lomax's shoulder and held out a brochure. "Quick question, sir. Is the Empire State Building all it's cracked up to be? Or is it just a tourist trap?"

"Could you stop talking for two seconds?" Lomax asked. "I'm in the middle of something very important."

"Can do," Tim said.

"Ask the officer if he wants some pop," Steffi called from the kitchenette.

"Would you care for a beverage?" Tim asked.

Lomax bristled. He made a sharp swerve to the right, intentionally throwing Tim against the Winnebago's door.

"I'll take that as a no," Tim said, rubbing his head.

"Can you pick up the pace?" Roxy asked. The Winnebago was gaining on them.

"Look, do you want to drive?" Jane snapped.

The car made a quick right turn. Roxy checked her side-view mirror. No more Winnebago. "Where did he go?" she asked.

Jane glanced at the rearview mirror. "Pretty sure we gave him the slip," she said.

"Uh, you may want to look to your right," the man in the back seat suggested.

The Winnebago pulled alongside them like a whale. Lomax's voice roared from the loudspeaker. "Playtime's over. Let's put the toys away and go home."

No way, Roxy thought. Lomax didn't have her yet. "Swerve left!" she told Jane.

Jane yanked the wheel left and screeched in front of a wave of oncoming traffic. Behind them the man in the suit screamed, "My coffee! Ahhh!"

Roxy glanced back. The man was being jostled around in the back seat. His cup lay on the floor, and his lap was covered with hot coffee. "Sorry, man," she said. Then she turned around and looked ahead. They were driving north, not south. "You're going the wrong way!" she cried to Jane. "Times Square is that way!" She frantically jabbed her hand in the opposite direction.

"I have it under control," Jane said through clenched teeth, sounding as if she was just about to lose it.

But Roxy knew they had to get off this street. The Winnebago was close enough to bump them, and a red light loomed ahead. She spotted a narrow alley off to the left. "Turn!" she yelled at Jane.

Jane turned hard—too hard. The cab cut off an oncoming car and spun halfway around. Then Roxy noticed a One Way sign—pointing the wrong way.

Jane put the car into reverse and zoomed into the alley backward. The man in the back seat screamed again.

"Hang on, people!" Jane cried.

Reinaldo whined, and Roxy held him tightly as the cab zoomed backward though the alley.

Then the Winnebago turned into the alley and tried to ram its way through. "You're mine now, Ryan!" Lomax called over the speaker.

"Faster!" Roxy cried.

"It's too tight," Tim said. "We're not going to make it!" The Winnebago's sides scraped against the walls of the alley. Sparks flew as metal crunched against brick.

"We'll make it," Lomax said. Then the camper ground to a halt. He stepped on the gas, hard. The camper wouldn't budge. It was stuck in the alley like a pig in a blanket.

The cab sped through the alley, spun out, righted itself, and zoomed down another street. Lomax pushed open the Winnebago's sun roof and popped his head out, watching the cab disappear.

Gone. Slipped out of his grasp again.

Lomax was down but not out. He knew he could still catch Ryan. He sat down and started backing the vehicle out of the alley.

"Where to now?" Tim asked.

"Times Square, folks," Lomax replied.

The way Tim and Steffi Brooger perked up annoyed him.

"Oh! Times Square, honey!" Tim said.

"I'll get the camera," Steffi said.

Lomax looked away in disgust. Tourists!

Jane glanced in her rearview mirror. No sign of the Winnebago. Lomax must not have made it through the alley. She pumped her fist in victory. "Yes! Take that!"

"You almost got us killed back there!" Roxy said.

Since when was Roxy Miss Careful? "Perfect time for criticism, Roxy," Jane said. She felt confident after her big car chase.

"Welcome to my planet," Roxy said. "Now you know how I feel."

"What's that supposed to mean?" Jane asked.

"Come on," Roxy said. "You're always looking down at me."

"What?" Jane swerved to the curb and stopped the cab. She heard their passenger tumbling around in the back seat. "Looking down at you! I've been looking *out* for you!"

The man opened the cab door and bolted out. "Thanks for nothing!" he shouted.

Whatever. Jane didn't care about him. She just couldn't believe that Roxy didn't appreciate how hard she worked to take care of the family, while all Roxy did was run around having fun!

"You've been looking out for me?" Roxy cried. "Tell me, how have you been looking out for me?"

"Are you insane?" Jane snapped. "It's all I ever do! And the *one* day I don't, the one day I actually try to do something for myself, I wind up hauled into the Roxy Ryan School of Juvenile Delinquency."

"I've been trying to help you from the minute we left the house!" Roxy said.

"A lot of good that's done," Jane said. They'd done nothing all day but run away from the trouble Roxy had caused. Jane wasn't going to take another minute of it. She had an important appointment to make and she wasn't going to let Roxy get in her way. She picked up Reinaldo, opened the door and stepped out of the cab. "I'm out of here."

Roxy jumped out of the cab and followed Jane. She wasn't going to let Jane walk away from this. She was going to make Jane see her side for once!

"Where are you going?" Roxy demanded. "I'm not finished!"

"Well, I am," Jane shot back. "Why don't you just run along and have fun. That's what you're good at, right?"

Roxy seethed. How dare she? "As opposed to what you're good at—which is walking away whenever we start to have a real conversation."

Jane spun around angrily. "I don't have time for real conversations! I'm too busy taking care of things."

"So who asked you to?" Roxy said.

"You did, the minute you stopped taking responsibility for anything after Mom died!"

At the word *Mom*, Roxy felt a wave of sadness wash over her. "That's so unfair."

Jane wouldn't let up. "You're right, it is. I might actually have a life if for once you'd start acting more like—"

She stopped. Roxy waited for her to finish the sentence, but she didn't.

"More like what?" she asked. Still no response. Jane looked uncomfortable. Well too bad. *She'd* brought it up, whatever it was. "You know, I'm not just another thing in your day planner to check off. I don't need you to keep me in line. I just need you to support me for who I am—which, among other things, is *not you!* We're different, Jane. And you know what I miss most about Mom? She loved that about us. You punish me for it. Since the day she died, you've done nothing but push me out of your life."

"I have not!" Jane looked genuinely startled, as if this thought were completely new to her.

"Oh, come off it, Jane. 'Biggest day of your academic career' and you didn't even bother to invite me."

"Well, forgive me for wanting one day to be about me for a change," Jane said. "Despite what you may think, Rox, they're not real easy to come by. I make honor roll, and Dad doesn't notice because *you're* in detention. I'm elected captain of the cheerleading squad, and Dad can't make one game because he has to go to *your* parent-counselor meetings. You know why I want this fellowship to study abroad? Because it's three thousand miles away from you!"

Jane's words hit Roxy like a punch in the gut. Roxy knew she got on Jane's nerves once in awhile. But she never knew Jane felt like this. The blood drained from her face.

"Well, I really hope you get it then," Roxy said quietly. She walked away, hurt to the core. If Jane didn't want her around, Roxy would leave her alone. Simple as that.

11

Jane held Reinaldo and watched Roxy walk down the street. *Why did I say that?* she wondered. *The last thing I wanted to do was to hurt my sister.* Her heart ached at the sight of Roxy looking so lonely. As soon as the words had popped out of her mouth she'd wanted to take them back.

But it was too late, and she didn't have time to fix it just then. She had to get her day planner back and race up to Columbia to give her speech. First things first.

She started walking downtown toward 47th Street and Broadway to meet Bennie, but she couldn't stop thinking about Roxy.

"She's got it all wrong," Jane said to Reinaldo. "And she said plenty of mean things to me too. What's all that about pushing her away? I don't push her away, right?"

Reinaldo let out a little doggy groan.

"I don't!" Jane insisted. She sighed and stroked his head. She had grown to like the little guy, ugly as he was. It was funny how she'd always disliked dogs, but now she didn't anymore. At least she didn't dislike *this* dog.

The microchip was still inside him. She knew Bennie would try to take Reinaldo from her. She would just have to find a way around it—somehow.

"Don't you worry," she said to Reinaldo. "I'm not going to let that mean man hurt one hair on your head." She stopped and looked around. She'd arrived at Broadway and 47th Street, but there was no sign of a long black limo. "Where is he?"

A small U-Haul moving truck was parked by the curb, its back doors wide open. It sat unattended, which was strange. New Yorkers didn't usually leave trucks wide open without watching them carefully.

Jane ambled closer. The truck was nearly empty, except for something small and black that lay on the floor. Her day planner!

Suspicious, Jane scanned the area for Bennie. "Hello?" she called out. She peered into the van and shouted out again, "Hello?"

No answer. No sign of Bennie.

"I wonder where he is," she said to the dog. "Maybe we lucked out. Maybe we can get away with the day planner *and* you, Reinaldo."

She set him down on the floor of the truck and climbed inside to grab her day planner.

She picked it up. It didn't feel right—too light. And it didn't look right—too new. She opened it. It was blank inside, except for a note: ANCIENT CHINESE PROVERB: NEVER ENTER EMPTY TRUCK ALONE.

Jane gasped and dropped the planner. She snatched up Reinaldo and lunged for the door. Bennie blocked her exit. He smiled at her and slammed the truck doors closed.

"Help!" Jane screamed. She tried to open the doors, but they were locked.

Reinaldo howled.

"Help!" Jane yelled, pounding on the doors. "Roxy!"

"Stupid Jane," Roxy muttered. She kicked an empty soda can as she shuffled down the street. She hated to admit how much her sister had hurt her. She wanted to be cool. But there was no denying it, when Jane said she wanted to be three thousand miles away from her, it cut her to the heart.

"I thought I knew her," she said to herself. "She's my sister! I mean, I know we've had some fights over the years. We're not much alike. But I always thought that deep down she loved me, even liked me! It really seemed that way. But I guess she doesn't. No wonder she's been pushing me out of her life."

She walked for blocks and blocks, staring at the sidewalk and thinking. Finally she looked up to see where she was. Big neon billboards flashed overhead. Crowds blocked the sidewalks and cars honked in the streets. Times Square.

This is where Jane was supposed to meet Bennie, Roxy thought. She spotted his familiar limo parked down the street.

She walked up to the limo and peered inside. She couldn't see through the tinted windows, so she opened the back door. Jane's day planner lay on the seat.

"Great," Roxy said, picking up the day planner. "Here's her stupid nerd book. I wonder where she is? And where's Bennie?"

She closed the door and started to walk away, but something stopped her. Did she just hear a bang? She moved toward the sound at the back of the limo. A muffled pounding sound—it came from the trunk!

She put an ear to the trunk. She heard someone crying "Help! Help!" as if through a mouthful of cotton. Someone was in there!

"Hello?" Roxy said, knocking on the top of the trunk with her knuckles.

"Roxy?" The voice was louder now. "Help!"

It sounded like Trey!

Roxy pushed a latch and popped open the trunk. Trey lay on the floor, his hair and clothes disheveled, gasping for breath.

He crawled out and gripped Roxy by the shoulders. "Thanks," he said.

"What were you doing in there?" Roxy asked.

"I don't know," Trey said. "One minute I'm coming to find you, and the next thing I know some psycho shoves me in here."

Roxy shook her head, horrified. "Just when I think it can't get any worse—" She walked over to a bench and plopped down on it. Nothing was going right. Nothing!

Trey looked at Roxy's face. She glanced away. "Hey—are you okay?" he asked.

"Yeah, I guess," Roxy said. Her breath got shaky as if she might start crying. *Can't have that*, she thought. *Better to talk than to cry in front of Trey*. "Not really," she admitted. "I just had a huge fight with my sister."

"Isn't that sort of normal for you two?" Trey asked.

"Yeah, but this was different. The kind of stuff you can't really take back." At the memory of Jane's words, Roxy felt hurt all over again. Then cynicism pushed away her sadness, and the anger came rushing back. "Not that she'd want to take it back," she added. "Anyway, it doesn't matter. Let her think what she wants. I really don't care."

"You sure about that?" Trey asked.

When Roxy really thought about it, she had to admit that she had caused Jane a few problems in her life. She didn't mean to, not at all . . . but some of the bad things that had happened that day *were* her fault. Maybe Jane had a right to be upset. . . .

And Jane really *did* try to help Roxy, in lots of little ways, like making sure she was awake in the morning and fixing Roxy her favorite breakfast even though it wasn't nutritious. . . . Maybe in a way Jane understood Roxy better than she thought.

Roxy smiled a little. Trey could see right through her. She liked that in a guy. The whole story came rushing out.

"So basically you see Jane as trying to run your life, and she sees you as trying to ruin hers," Trey said after she had finished.

"In a nutshell, yeah," Roxy said. "The thing is, even if I told her it wasn't true, that I really do care, she'd never believe me."

"So maybe you need to show her that you care instead," Trey suggested.

Roxy shook her head. "It's too late. She was supposed to give this major speech today, and now she's going to lose that fellowship because there's no way she'll get there on time, and it's the most important thing in the world to her. . . ."

Roxy glanced down at the day planner. A thought suddenly occurred to her. She opened the book. There were the note cards for Jane's speech. "How would you like to go on a little field trip?" she asked Trey.

"Sounds good," Trey said. "By the way, where's Reinaldo?"

"Jane has him," Roxy admitted.

"I've got to find him," Trey said. "My mother must be losing her mind."

"I've got to find Jane," Roxy added. "I hope she's all right. She's supposed to be here, but she's not."

"Where else could she be?" Trey asked.

"I don't know." Roxy flipped through Jane's planner and stopped on that day's date.

In Jane's neat handwriting, it said McGILL FELLOWSHIP, COLUMBIA U., 3:00 P.M., METGER HALL.

"Wherever she is, at some point she's bound to end up at Columbia," Roxy said, standing up. She took Trey by the hand and led him back toward Mickey's cab. "Come on—we're going uptown!"

"Where is he taking us?" Jane wondered aloud as she sat in the dark U-Haul cabin. The truck bumped over the streets, making sudden, jarring stops. Jane held Reinaldo. He whined and licked her hand.

At last the door opened, and sunshine flooded the truck. Bennie grabbed her roughly by one arm and pulled her out. "Come on," he said. "This dog has a date with Ma."

"Ma?" Jane muttered. "Who's Ma?"

Bennie snatched Reinaldo out of Jane's arms and pushed her across the sidewalk toward a salon. MA BANG'S NAIL PARLOR, the sign read. Inside the dingy nail salon one customer was having a manicure. Bennie led Jane to a kitchen in the back. An old Chinese woman sat at a table, sipping tea.

"I've got them, Ma," Bennie said. He set Reinaldo on the table.

"Good," the old woman said. "Put her in the Hole."

"What?" Jane cried. The Hole? That didn't sound good. "You can't do this!" she shouted as Bennie dragged her away. "Don't you dare hurt that dog!"

"Quiet!" Bennie growled. He shoved her into a small dark room, shut the door and locked it.

Jane's eyes slowly adjusted to the darkness. She looked around. The Hole seemed to be some kind of storage room. Dust tickled Jane's throat and she coughed. An extremely dirty storage room, piled high with CDs, DVDs, cheap handbags, watches, computer equipment, and cardboard boxes.

How am I ever going to get out of here? Jane

thought. *If only Roxy had been with me. She would have figured out something.*

She sat on the floor, fighting off tears. She had to bust out of there somehow, and fast, before Bennie and Ma sliced open Reinaldo to get that chip! What did they want it so badly for anyway?

She rose to her feet and looked at one of the handbags. It looked like a designer purse, but the logo wasn't quite right. All this stuff must be counterfeit!

She opened one of the boxes. Inside were stacks and stacks of CDs. Jane dumped them onto the floor and studied them. The covers were clearly color photocopies, not real CD covers. She picked up a CD. *This album hasn't been released yet*, she realized. Neither had the DVDs.

They're fakes, Jane realized. She remembered an article she'd seen in the newspaper that morning. Roxy had even made a comment about it. Something about music piracy . . .

So that was what Bennie and Ma were up to. The chip must contain stolen music. They copied it onto CDs and sold them before the real albums were released, ripping off the record companies!

She paced the room, pressing against the walls, searching for a way out. There was a lot of money at stake, and Bennie and Ma didn't care if a dog had to die so they could get their hands on it. And what would they do with her? She had to get out of there! But there were no windows, only the thick steel door, which Bennie had locked.

Her pacing kicked up a cloud of dust. She coughed, waving it away. In a corner she spotted a DustBuster.

Whew! Got to get rid of some of this dust before I suffocate! Jane thought. She turned on the DustBuster and started vacuuming. *Wow! This thing is surprisingly heavy.* Then she stopped and smiled. Maybe *that* was a way out. . . .

"Now it's just you and me," Bennie said. "Alone. Nowhere to hide." Reinaldo stood on the kitchenette table in front of him. Bennie stared into the dog's eyes.

"Bennie!" Ma Bang stood in the doorway, watching him. "Is this your idea of torture? You're wasting my time. Just slice him open and get it over with."

Bennie nodded, but he didn't want to cut

open the dog if he didn't have to. Secretly he hated the sight of blood.

Ma walked toward Reinaldo. "Cats have nine lives," she said. "I wonder if dogs do too. . . ."

Suddenly a loud banging sound came from the Hole. "It's that girl!" Ma said. "What is she doing? Make her stop! I'll handle the mutt."

Bennie started from the room. He stopped to glance back at Reinaldo. Ma took out a sharp nail file and crept up to the dog. "Now we'll do it my way," she said. She looked up at Bennie and snapped, "You heard me! Go!"

Bennie hurried to the Hole and unlocked the door. The banging was louder than ever. "What's going on in here?"

It worked! Jane stopped banging the DustBuster against the metal door. *He's coming in!* As the door creaked open, Jane shrank behind a stack of shelves and gripped a metal chain that hung from a track on the ceiling.

"Hey, give me a break." Bennie stepped into the room. "Or my mom's going to—"

"Ahhhh!" Jane swung out from behind the

shelves and crashed into Bennie, knocking him to the floor. She pushed over the shelves and ran to the kitchen.

"Ow!" she heard Ma shout. "He bit me!"

Reinaldo was growling. *Good going, boy,* Jane thought. She dashed into the kitchen. Ma was bent over in pain, holding her bitten hand.

"Reinaldo, are you coming?" Jane called.

The dog leaped into her arms, and she darted out of the kitchen before Ma could stop her. She slammed the door shut and locked it behind her.

That takes care of them for now, Jane thought. She raced out of the nail salon, glancing at a clock on the wall. Two-thirty! She was supposed to give her presentation at Columbia at three!

She ran into the street and stuck out her arm to hail a cab. "Taxi! Taxi!" she yelled. She looked around. She was on a small street in Chinatown, no taxis in sight.

Then she saw him. Across the street, wheeling his bike out of an electronics shop. Jim! That handsome, adorable guy! And his bike! His speedy, traffic-dodging bike!

She hurried over to him. "Jim!" she cried. "How would you like to save my life?"

"I could do that," he said with a smile.

Jane grabbed his wrist and looked at his watch. "I have exactly twenty-eight minutes and thirteen seconds to get to Columbia University. That's a hundred and twenty-one blocks from here. What do you think? Can we make it?"

"In a New York minute." Jim hopped onto his bike. "You'd better hold on," he said.

Jane hopped on behind him. She put her arms around his waist, and he started pedaling. "Columbia University, here we come!"

12

Roxy squealed to a stop in front of the main gate at Columbia University. She jumped out of Mickey's cab, leaving it parked by the curb. Trey climbed out of the passenger seat.

"Where are we going?" Trey asked.

"Metger Hall," Roxy said. She spotted a sign that said METGER HALL and had an arrow pointing across the quad. "This way!"

They raced across campus. Roxy had to find Jane. If she hadn't made it to her scholarship presentation, then where was she?

"There it is." Trey pointed at a large brick building. They ran up the steps and into a grand auditorium. Roxy stopped to take it in.

It was a huge, high-ceilinged hall filled to capacity with students, professors, and administrators. A wooden balcony ran along the sides and the back.

A preppy young man in a blue blazer stood on the stage, behind a podium with a microphone, speaking to the audience.

"This would serve the underlying principles of a free-market society," the young man said. "Thank you."

The audience applauded as he left the stage. Roxy grabbed Trey's wrist and read his watch. It was almost three o'clock. Jane was supposed to be up next. Where was she?

"Maybe there's a waiting room or something backstage," Trey suggested.

"Good thinking," Roxy said. She left the auditorium and ran down a hallway, searching for Jane. She slid to a stop in front of an open door. In a small room a dozen students sat in chairs, studying note cards just like Jane's. This had to be the place.

"Jane!" Roxy called into the room. The students looked up at her. No Jane. Now she was really worried. Jane would never miss this presentation—not if she could help it. Where was she?

A man walked into the room with a clipboard. "Jane Ryan? Jane Ryan?"

No one answered. *Jane's missing her big chance*, Roxy thought. *If she doesn't make that speech, she won't get to go to Oxford University. But she's not here to make it.*

But Roxy was there. She gripped the day planner in her hand. The note cards were in there—with Jane's speech written on them. *If I make the speech in Jane's place, at least she'll still have a shot at that scholarship. She'll probably be mad when she finds out, but what's the worst she can do to me?*

"Jane Ryan!" the man called again.

"Here I am," Roxy said.

"You're on next," the man said.

"Do you know what you're doing?" Trey asked.

Roxy nodded. "I got her into this mess. I'm going to get her out of it. Besides, how hard can reading a bunch of note cards be?"

Trey didn't say a word, but he looked doubtful.

"Go with me on this," Roxy said.

Trey broke into a smile. "Hey, you're going to be great." He gave her a kiss on the cheek. "See you in the auditorium."

Roxy watched him walk over to the auditorium's main doors. She started toward the stage door, then stopped. She was still wearing the red sequined dress and matching jacket from Big Shirl's House of Bling. Not exactly appropriate. She needed something to nerd herself up a bit. . . .

She glanced around the waiting room. A girl with shiny black hair was sitting in an armchair, reading the *Wall Street Journal*. Roxy took in her preppy blue blazer, complete with a nametag that said MUFFIE. Muffie didn't need the blazer anymore—she was finished with her speech, and it would make the perfect cover-up for Roxy's blinged-out dress.

"Nice blazer, Muffie," Roxy said. "Want to trade?"

Muffie smiled. *Ah*, *yes*, Roxy thought, removing her red sequined jacket. *I believe we have a customer.*

"Mother!" Trey stopped dead in his tracks inside the auditorium, shocked. Senator Lipton was sitting in the front row, a clipboard in her lap. "What are you doing here?"

"I'm honorary chair of the McGill Fellowship committee," Senator Lipton said.

"What are *you* doing here? I thought you were picking up Reinaldo."

Trey fumbled for an excuse. Why would he be at Columbia to see a bunch of high school kids vie for a scholarship? He wouldn't—unless Roxy was one of the contestants. And she wasn't—not really.

"I am picking him up, very soon. But I, uh, wanted to . . ." *Think, Trey, think!* "I wanted to see you present the award, of course," he finally said.

The senator smiled and gave her son a hug. "First you take Reinaldo to the groomer, then you surprise your mother," she said. "I'm not sure whether to be touched or suspicious."

Trey smiled. "Sorry, Mom—I can't help you. You're going to have to figure that out for yourself."

"Our next finalist hails from Long Island," the moderator said as Roxy watched from the wings, wearing the borrowed blazer over her glam dress and clutching Jane's day planner. "She holds a four-point-two grade point average," the moderator continued. "In addition she's student body president and captain of her high school cheerleading squad. Please welcome Jane Ryan."

The audience applauded and Roxy stepped out onto the stage. *Whoops!* The day planner slipped out of her hand and dropped to the floor. Roxy quickly scooped it up and hurried to the podium.

She smiled, trying to look confident. The crowd stared at her, waiting. She opened the day planner, looking for Jane's note cards. She knew they had to be in there somewhere. She flipped through the pages. No note cards. No speech. Where was it? "Oh, no," she muttered.

Roxy cast a nervous glance at the panel of judges seated in the front row. Two professor-looking ladies, an old man in a bow tie, Trey *(How did he get such a good seat?)*, that senator lady *(Gulp! Trey's mother! Reinaldo's mommy!)*, and a blondish-gray-haired executive-type with a black eye holding a cup of coffee . . .

Roxy gasped. It was him! The guy from the train, the hotel, and the taxi! Who kept spilling coffee on himself!

He stopped scribbling on his clipboard and looked up to take a sip from his cup. He noticed Roxy standing at the podium. Roxy could see him clamp his lips shut to keep from spitting coffee all over his lap.

"Oh. My. God," Roxy murmured.

The man swallowed his coffee and smiled. *He's getting a kick out of this,* Roxy thought, her nervousness growing. *He's going to enjoy watching me roast like a pig on a spit. Maybe I'd better get out of here.*

She started to step away from the podium, but the moderator said, "You may proceed, Miss Ryan."

There was no going back now. Roxy plastered a smile onto her face and paged through the day planner again, trying to buy some time.

"Please begin, Miss Ryan," one of the judges said.

Roxy cleared her throat. She was just going to have to wing it. *Here goes nothing.* "As many of you know, economy is very important. Take the word *economy*. When you break it down you have *eco*, which stands for the environment, which we're all in support of, and *onomy*, which is pig Latin for *money*. That being said, without economy in our lives we would all be . . ." She paused, searching for something intelligent-sounding to say. "Economically challenged." She paused again. *I'm not doing so badly*, she thought.

Trey clapped, but no one else did. His mother shot him a disapproving look and he stopped and slumped in his seat.

"Thank you," Roxy said. *Just act as if you know what you're doing, and they'll fall for it*, Roxy told herself. It had worked for her many times before. Still, she had a feeling this time might be different.

She flipped desperately through the day planner, hoping for some inspiration. She wanted to help Jane, not spoil her chances.

She glanced back toward the wings, where she'd dropped the day planner. That's when she saw them—a little pile of papers in rainbow colors. The note cards! They must have fallen out when she dropped the day planner. Was it too late to run across the stage and pick them up?

"Miss Ryan, please continue," a judge said. "We're running short of time."

Oh, well, Roxy thought. *I guess Jane Ryan's speech will just have to have a lot of Roxy in it.*

"Here we are!" Jim called.

Jane and Reinaldo held on tight as Jim's

bike zipped onto the Columbia campus and tore across the quad. Jane couldn't believe how fast Jim could pedal with a passenger on his bike. They'd made it uptown in record time.

Jim flashed his watch at her and asked, "How are we doing for time?"

Jane looked at his watch. It was three o'clock exactly. "It's going to be tight," she said.

Metger Hall was just ahead. "That's it!" she shouted. Jim rode right up to the building. Jane jumped off the bike and flew up the steps. She just hoped she wasn't too late.

The auditorium doors were closed. Jane paused in front of them to straighten her mod jumper. She hadn't planned on wearing a party dress to the presentation, but it was too late to worry about that now.

Jim held Reinaldo for her. "Just out of curiosity, how do I look?" she asked.

Jim smiled. "You look amazing."

She took a deep breath. She didn't have her day planner, but strangely, it didn't matter. She remembered her speech perfectly without it. Maybe she didn't need the book so much after all.

She threw open the auditorium doors and headed down the aisle. A girl stood at the podium, speaking. Jane didn't pay much attention to her at first. *That must be the girl scheduled to speak before me*, she thought. *Maybe I lucked out for once and they're running late.*

But the girl's voice sounded weirdly familiar. Jane looked up at her. Her jaw dropped open. It was Roxy!

"For as the famous Canadian economist, Professor Avril Lavigne-stein, once said, and I quote, 'Why must we go and make things so complicated?'" Roxy was saying.

I can't believe she's doing this for me, Jane thought. She knew Roxy would never get on a stage to deliver a speech just for fun. She was filling in for Jane—and trying to salvage her scholarship!

Roxy noticed Jane approaching from the back. "Jane!" she cried happily. "Thank God!"

Jane hurried down the aisle toward the podium. Jim and Reinaldo followed her.

"Well, folks," Roxy said into the microphone. "That's my time. And now, would the real Jane Ryan please stand up? Ah, look—here she is now!"

Maybe I still have a chance, Jane thought, passing the front row. Suddenly Senator Lipton shot up and cried, "Reinaldo! What are you doing here?"

Jane stopped short. *Is Senator Lipton one of the judges?*

Trey stood beside her. "Hey, look at that, Mom," he said. "The dog groomer delivers!"

Jane pretended she didn't hear that and hurried up the steps to the podium. Behind her the crowd murmured restlessly.

"Are you okay?" Roxy whispered. "I didn't know what happened to you!"

"I'm fine," Jane said. "What are you doing here?"

"Well, apart from totally humiliating myself onstage . . . I'm so sorry. I wanted to read your speech for you—"

"Actually, from what I heard, yours was way more entertaining," Jane said. She smiled at Roxy's stunned look. *Roxy thought I was going to be mad at her. She has no idea how grateful I am!* "I can take it from here," she said and stepped up to the podium.

The bright lights beamed into her eyes, blinding her. Jane had been here before, many times, in her nightmares. The ones where she forgot to put on her clothes. She glanced down at her House of Bling outfit. Whew! She wasn't naked. Big Shirl's clothes were a lot better than nothing.

Roxy took Reinaldo from Jim and walked into the wings to watch Jane's speech.

"Ladies and gentlemen," Jane began. "I am Jane Ryan." She glanced across the stage to mouth *thanks* to Roxy when something caught her eye. Someone was moving behind her sister. Then the figure stepped into the light. Lomax!

13

"Roxy, behind you!" Jane shouted.

Lomax grabbed Roxy and marched her out onto the stage. A buzz tore through the crowd. What was going on?

Jane's heart sank. How could Lomax do this to them—now of all times?

Lomax flashed his badge. "Nassau County Department of Truancy. Roxanne Ryan is now in my custody. And this girl"— he pointed at Jane—"is an accomplice to her sister's criminal activities."

The buzz in the crowd became a roar.

"He's right!" a voice boomed from the right of the stage. Jane turned her head. Bennie and Ma! "That girl stole my mutt!" Bennie shouted, pointing at Reinaldo.

Senator Lipton leaped to her feet. "I don't know what's going on here, but that 'mutt' happens to be mine, and I am ordering you to leave him alone!"

Jane closed her eyes. How could this be happening to her? It made her nightmare look good!

Bennie stepped toward the edge of the stage, threatening Senator Lipton. "Yeah? You and what army?"

Senator Lipton pointed to Roxy, who held Reinaldo. "Officer, would you let go of the girl?" she commanded.

Lomax looked confused. "Let go of her? Why, Senator?"

"To stop that thief!" Senator Lipton shouted, pointing at Bennie.

Jane saw Lomax hesitate. She knew how hard it must be for him to let Roxy go after trying so hard to catch her. But the senator had just called him Officer, and that had to mean a lot to him too. And, after all, what was more important: catching a student cutting school or nabbing a real criminal?

"Officer, are you going to obey my order?" Senator Lipton demanded.

"Yes, ma'am!" Lomax let Roxy go and took off after Bennie, who ran off the stage and barreled through the crowd.

Now was Jane's chance to get something off her chest. She'd been thinking about Roxy since their fight and had something important to say to her. She grabbed her by one arm.

"Maybe we should go," Roxy said.

"No. I need to say something right here and now," Jane insisted. "And this is what I want to say: Thank you."

"You mean, you're not mad?" Roxy asked.

"Are you kidding?" Jane said. "It was so cool of you to try to save my scholarship." She paused. Here came the hard part. "Rox, I'm sorry about all those things I said earlier. I was just having a meltdown because everything seemed to be going wrong."

"And each time I tried to fix it, it just got worse," Roxy admitted.

"But none of it was your fault," Jane said. "And you were right about what you said in the sewer."

"Water main," Roxy corrected her.

"Whatever," Jane said. There was a clatter at the foot of the stage. Jane looked down to see Lomax catching up to Bennie. "The point is, you were right. We haven't spent a day together in a long time. And I've really missed that," Jane said.

"I've missed you too," Roxy said.

Reinaldo trotted up to them and licked Roxy's leg. Roxy picked him up.

Jane heard a crash and looked out into the audience. It was total chaos! Lomax was chasing Bennie and Ma, people were screaming and knocking chairs over trying to get out of their way.

Senator Lipton ran after Lomax, shouting, "Get him, Officer! Get him!"

"Let's make a run for it," Roxy said.

"No," Jane said. "No more running." It was time to stop this madness and face the consequences. Jane stepped up to the podium and grabbed the microphone.

"Um, excuse me everyone! Quiet!" she called.

No one listened. People were shouting and fighting and throwing punches. The place was a madhouse!

"FREEZE, PEOPLE!" Jane shouted.

It worked. Everyone stopped dead in their tracks and turned their heads toward Jane. There, that was much better.

"I think I can explain what's going on here," Jane said. "That man—" She pointed to Bennie, who was standing on a windowsill, trying to squeeze his massive body through the opening, without success. "That guy and his mother," Jane continued, pointing out Ma Bang cowering in a corner of the room, "are criminals dealing in pirated music, movies, and maybe even Gucci handbags."

The crowd gasped. Jane spotted Senator Lipton at the edge of the stage, reaching for Reinaldo.

Roxy handed the dog to her.

"As I recall, Senator," Jane said, "your campaign for re-election includes a pledge to crack down on digital fraud. So I'm sure you'll agree that this is one heck of a score for you. As for evidence, I suggest the next time you take Reinaldo for a walk, you look closely at anything he leaves behind."

Senator Lipton glanced at Reinaldo and wrinkled her nose in distaste. "And how, may I ask, did you two girls become involved in all of this?" she asked.

Jane opened her mouth to reply, but Lomax stepped forward. "Senator, allow me to shed some light—"

Jane cut him off. "The truth is, Senator, it was this crime fighter—Officer Lomax—who tracked down the Bang family. He refused to rest until justice was served. We're just witnesses to his sting operation." *That ought to help get Roxy off the hook*, she thought.

Roxy nodded. "Yeah, what she said."

"Is this true, Officer Lomax?" the senator asked. "You engineered this collar?"

Lomax glanced at Roxy, then back at the senator. "I don't want to gloat, but the word *mastermind* comes to mind."

Yes! Jane thought. *It worked! He's going to give up on Roxy for a chance to be a real cop!*

"Well, I'll see to it that you get the highest commendation," Senator Lipton promised.

The room began to settle down. Lomax yanked Bennie out of the open window and put him in handcuffs. "Hey, you aren't even a real cop," Bennie complained.

"Zip it, Odd Job," Lomax snapped. "Thanks to you, that's all about to change."

Jane picked up her day planner, which was lying on the podium where Roxy had left it. Now that she finally had it back, she couldn't remember why she'd needed it so badly. She flipped it open. *That's weird. My note cards aren't in here*, she thought. *Oh, well, it doesn't matter anyway. It's too late for my speech. The fellowship is history.*

Jane took Roxy's hand, and they stepped off the stage, ready to go home at last. "I'm still sorry the day didn't work out the way you planned," Roxy said.

"Until now I felt the same way." Jane held up her day planner. "That's the whole point of these things—to make sure everything goes as planned, no surprises. The problem is, they don't take into account those little accidents that end up being little miracles." She hugged Roxy.

"Mom would've been proud of you," Roxy whispered.

"She would've been proud of both of us," Jane whispered back.

They made their way through the dispersing crowd. Lomax had caught Ma Bang and was handcuffing her to Bennie.

Senator Lipton passed Reinaldo's leash to Trey. "Well, then," she said, "let's go see if Reinaldo is ready to give up some evidence. I'll let you do the honors, Trey." She marched toward the exit.

Trey followed with Reinaldo in tow. He glanced back at Roxy, holding a hand to his ear like a phone. *Can I call you?* he mouthed.

Jane glanced at Roxy, even though she

knew what her sister would say. Roxy smiled and gave him a thumbs up.

Whoops! While she was watching Roxy, Jane bumped into somebody. She turned around. It was Jim. Again. He grinned at her. The way his eyes crinkled at the corners made Jane melt. *He's so cute*, she thought.

"It was, um, really nice bumping into you today," she said.

"Maybe we could bump again," Jim said. Jane raised an eyebrow. He gave her a funny look. "Did I just say that out loud?"

Jane nodded. "Yeah, and I'm glad you did." She reached up and kissed him, long and sweetly. *Wow!* Jane thought.

Something beeped, and they broke apart. Jim blushed. "It's just my alarm watch," he said, switching it off. Jane grinned. He had one just like hers!

"I'll call you later," Jim promised. He waved to Roxy, gave Jane another quick kiss, and left.

"Look what we've accomplished today!" Jane said to Roxy. "We captured two of the most wanted criminals!"

Roxy smiled. "Still, I'm sorry about the fellowship. I guess that's a lost cause now."

Jane shrugged. "Everything happens for a reason. Maybe Oxford University just wasn't meant to be."

Buzzzz! Jane bolted up in bed and slapped her alarm clock. The buzzing stopped. She'd just had a terrible dream. She was giving a speech to the McGill Fellowship committee when she looked down and realized she was naked!

Hey, didn't I have that dream yesterday? she wondered. *And the day before that? And the day before that? The big day has passed. Shouldn't these recurring nightmares stop now?*

She put on her glasses and looked around. She was safe in her room. The McGill Fellowship presentation had been the day before, and it had turned out even worse than she'd dreamed. The weird thing was she wasn't that upset about it.

The day before, if you'd told Jane the McGill presentation would end in total disaster she would have wanted to curl up and die, but today it just didn't seem that important to her.

Still, it would be nice to go to Oxford University, she thought. She couldn't deny that she would have loved to win the scholarship.

Someone knocked on her door. "Come in," Jane called. The door opened, and Roxy backed into the room. "Roxy, I just had the weirdest dream—" Jane said. She gasped when Roxy turned around. Her sister was carrying a tray loaded with Jane's favorite breakfast foods—oatmeal, fruit salad, and coffee. Jane could hardly speak. She was always the one who made breakfast. Roxy had never done anything like this for her before.

"Good morning," Roxy said.

"It isn't my birthday," Jane said, grasping for reasons Roxy would bring her breakfast in bed.

"No, because then it would be my birthday too," Roxy reminded her. "I just thought you could use a day off. Here's your paper."

Roxy handed her the morning paper. "Interesting news day," she added.

Jane stared at the headline on the front page: MUSIC PIRATES APPREHENDED IN LOCAL BUST. A picture showed Lomax leading Bennie and Ma Bang out of a police van in handcuffs. There was another photo of Senator Lipton surrounded by hundreds of counterfeit CDs. The caption read: *Senator Leads Sting Operation.*

"Wow!" Jane said.

"By the way, Jim left a message asking if you and Trey and I want to get together with him tonight. Am I forgetting anything?"

"Um—" So many things were happening at once Jane could hardly think. She'd just woken up, she hadn't even gotten out of bed yet, and suddenly she realized she'd helped catch two dangerous criminals *and* she had a major new crush.

"Girls, can you come down here for a second?" their father called.

Still in her pajamas, Jane got out of bed and headed downstairs with Roxy. They found Dr. Ryan waiting for them in the living room. Jane stopped dead in her tracks when she saw who was with him.

The executive guy! The one who kept spilling coffee on himself! At least his black eye looked a little better today.

"Girls, is there anything about yesterday that you'd like to tell me?" Dr. Ryan asked sternly.

"Uhhh . . ." Where should she start? And what was this guy doing here, anyway? Who was he and why couldn't she seem to get away from him?

"Roxy?" Dr. Ryan said.

"Ahhhh . . ." Roxy stammered.

I guess we should apologize to this guy, Jane thought. *We put him through a lot yesterday.* "Look, sir," she began, "I'm really sorry about what happened yesterday, and—"

"It's okay," the man said, holding up a hand to stop her. "Just . . . let me do the talking here. First of all, allow me introduce myself. My name is Hudson McGill."

Jane gasped. "Of the McGill Fellowship?"

He nodded. "I can't say that yesterday was one of the proudest days of my life," he went on. "But it was certainly the most memorable."

Jane felt the blood drain from her face. What was he doing here? Had he come just to rub it in that she'd totally screwed up?

"I came to return something of yours," Hudson said.

Something of mine? Jane was confused. Why would Hudson McGill have something that belonged to her?

He held up a small pile of tattered, rainbow-colored note cards. "You see, I found these on the edge of the stage yesterday."

"My speech!" Jane cried.

"They fell out of your day planner when I dropped it," Roxy explained. "I didn't have time to pick them up."

"Well, I picked them up, once the chaos settled down," Hudson said, "and I read them with great interest. It's a fine speech, Jane. A brilliant speech, actually."

Jane's head began to spin. She could hardly believe this was happening.

"But what impressed me most is how you carried yourself up there on that stage yesterday," Hudson continued. "Poised. Confident. Resolved. Those are the qualities that impressed me the most." He stood up and handed her a certificate.

Jane read it aloud. "'This certifies that Jane Ryan has earned the McGill Fellowship, and as a Fellow, is entitled to four years of full tuition at Oxford University in Oxford, England.'" It was signed by Hudson McGill.

Jane looked at him in confusion. "But I thought . . ."

"There's nothing that says I can't grant a fellowship *after* the presentation," Hudson said. "After all, I am a McGill. Congratulations."

"Thank you!" Jane cried. She was so

happy she threw her arms around Hudson and hugged him.

"I'm very proud of you, Jane," Dr. Ryan said. He hugged her and then Roxy. "I'm proud of both of you." He turned to Hudson and added, "May I offer you some coffee?"

"No!" Hudson replied firmly.

Jane and Roxy giggled.

"I mean, no thank you," he said. "I've sworn off coffee for awhile, but I wouldn't mind some tea. *Iced* tea!"

"Come with me." Dr. Ryan led him into the kitchen.

Jane stayed behind with Roxy. She couldn't believe her luck! For once it was good—very, very good!

"You cool?" Roxy asked.

Jane beamed with happiness. "Oh, I'm very cool."

Roxy hugged her, and Jane squeezed back. "You're a great sister, Jane," Roxy said. "The best."

"So are you, Roxy," Jane said. "So are you."

"You look great, Jane," Roxy said. Jane walked out of the house dressed in a green blazer and jeans, carrying a travel tote bag. Their father trailed behind her, carrying a duffel bag. Roxy couldn't believe that a year had gone by already. So much had happened to them since the day of the McGill Fellowship presentation.

Roxy managed to finish high school without getting kicked out. Jane graduated with the highest honors, of course. And now Jane was all set to fly to England and start college. And Roxy . . .

"I'm going to miss you, Rox," Jane said.

"Hey, you're just a phone call away," Roxy said.

"A very expensive phone call," their father put in. Roxy threw him a mock-annoyed look. "What?" he said, shrugging. "With the way you two gab, I could be penniless in weeks."

Roxy and Jane laughed. Roxy hugged her sister tightly. Over the last year Jane had let Roxy back into her life. And she became part of Roxy's life too. Roxy was going to miss Jane more than ever, now that they were close again.

A bus horn beeped. Roxy pulled away and wiped a tear from her eye. She turned and waved at the bus. It was painted black, and printed on the side in giant silver letters were the words SIMPLE PLAN WORLD TOUR.

Roxy's friend Justin stuck his head out the window. "Yo, Roxy, we've got to go!" He waved and added, "Hi, Dr. Ryan. Hi, Jane."

Jane waved back.

"Morning, Justin," Dr. Ryan said.

Roxy took the travel tote from Jane and the duffel bag from her dad and walked toward the bus. She was sorry to leave Jane but excited too. Her dream had come true. Simple Plan's manager had hired Roxy and Justin to be roadies for the band's world tour. She was on her way to a life of rock 'n' roll!

"I'll see you in England in six weeks!" Jane called after her. "Good luck with the tour!"

Roxy gave her a thumbs up. "Maybe I'll work my way up from roadie to backup drummer," she said. "Who knows?"

Just then a police motorcycle pulled up in front of the bus. Roxy grinned and waved at the man driving the motorcycle—Officer Lomax. He'd finally been hired by the police force as a thanks for his brave capture of Bennie and Ma Bang. He didn't have time to bother with truant students anymore. He poured all his energy into catching real criminals now.

"Thought you might need a police escort out of town," Lomax said.

"Thanks, Officer Lomax," Roxy said.

"I'll take any excuse to use these." Lomax flipped on his siren and flashing cherry light.

Roxy laughed and boarded the bus. She gave one last wave to Jane as the bus pulled away. It drove off, and Roxy sighed happily, ready to face the future.

Everything had turned out great for Jane and great for her. Best of all, now she had more than a sister. She had a friend for life.

Mary-Kate and Ashley's

GRADUATION SUMMER

is about to begin!

Senior prom, graduation, saying good-bye to old friends and making new ones. For Mary-Kate and Ashley, this is the summer that will change their lives forever . . . *Graduation Summer*. And they can't wait!

NEW

Coming soon!
GRADUATION SUMMER
#1 We Can't Wait!
#2 Never Say Good-bye
#3 Everything I Want

mary-kateandashley

new york minute

We had our entire day planned… We thought! So how did we end up being chased all the way from Long Island through Chinatown to Harlem by police, politicians and an angry truant officer? We're still trying to figure it out!

ONE WAY

Play out all your favorite scenes from *New York Minute* with our Mary-Kate and Ashley fashion dolls!

ONE WAY

ONE WAY

Real Dolls for Real Girls

DUALSTAR
CONSUMER PRODUCTS

MATTEL

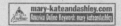